Books by Milton Hindus

The Crippled Giant, 1950
The Proustian Vision, 1954
Leaves of Grass: A Hundred Years After, 1955
A Reader's Guide to Marcel Proust, 1962
F. Scott Fitzgerald: An Introduction and Interpretation, 1967
The Old East Side, 1969
Walt Whitman: The Critical Heritage, 1971
A World at Twilight, 1971
Charles Reznikoff: A Critical Essay, 1977
The Worlds of Maurice Samuel, 1977
The Broken Music Box (Selected Poems), 1980
Charles Reznikoff: Man and Poet, 1984
The Crippled Giant (expanded edition), 1986
Essays: Personal and Impersonal, 1988

ESSAYS:
Personal and Impersonal

by

Milton Hindus

Black Sparrow Press
Santa Rosa
1988

LIBRARY OF CONGRESS CATALOGING-IN-PUBLICATION DATA

Hindus, Milton, 1916-
    Essays : personal and impersonal.

    Includes index.
    I. Title.
PS3558.I478E87   1988   809   87-24983
ISBN 0-87685-722-5 (alk. paper)
ISBN 0-87685-721-7 (pbk. : alk. paper)

I, on my side, require of every writer, first or last, a simple and sincere account of his own life, and not merely what he has heard of other men's lives; some such account as he would send to his kindred in a distant land, for if he has lived sincerely, it must have been in a distant land to me.

Henry David Thoreau, *Walden*

For no two people are measures identical . . . The critic who doesn't make a personal statement, in re measurements he himself has made, is merely an unreliable critic. He is not a measurer but a repeater of other men's results . . . KRINO, to pick out for oneself . . . to choose. That's what the word (critic) means.

Ezra Pound, *How To Read*

We must be resigned, but not too much so; we must be calm, but not too calm; we must not give in, yet we must give in some: that is, we must grade our rebellion and conformity both!

Walt Whitman, in conversation,
as quoted by Horace Traubel in
With Walt Whitman in Camden

Table of Contents

Prefatory Remarks
and Acknowledgments

THE COMBINATION OF so personal an effort as autobiography and such an impersonal one as criticism may seem unusual enough to require some explanation. The autobiographical segments here are parts of a larger book, which has been completed for over thirty years but which I have hesitated to publish in its entirety because there has always seemed the possibility of improving it and also because some of its contents are intimate enough to be embarrassing to a writer who has no greater claims to public attention than the author. It has been my conviction that the most truly sincere autobiographies must almost of necessity be those which are posthumously published. Both Dostoyevsky and Mark Twain are in agreement that it is not given to human nature to be entirely frank, open and objective about itself, and therefore though I was tempted by the challenge very early in life, I have long been of two minds about publishing the results.

The main focus here, in any case, is upon criticism, and the autobiographical revelations are present for whatever light they may shed upon the choice of subjects and the attitudes expressed in the criticism. So the chapter on the writer's Politics should be read in connection with the essays on Whittaker Chambers, on Walt Whitman, on Marcel Proust, and on Louis-Ferdinand Céline. My conviction is that the most important life is that of the mind, and if this does not transpire through all the writer's work, then indeed he has written in vain.

Most of the contents of this book has appeared in print before but so widely scattered that the separate pieces could not exert whatever weight and strength they may have together. They are representative samplings of the writer's diverse interests, but my hope is that they may all point to the presence of a single person behind them, rather unlike that whimsical horseman who has been humorously described

as galloping off in all directions. Perhaps the image I have of this book
is that of a racing shell with the separate essays serving as oarsmen,
who pull the boat to one side or another, while all together, directed
by the coxswain (who is none other than the author himself), they
make straight towards a single literary goal.

The initial piece of autobiography, *The Tombstone,* has not appeared in print before. Though it has been recently retouched, it was
substantially complete when the writer was still in his twenties. The
second selection served Doubleday as the Introduction to Maurice
Hindus's posthumously published book of memoirs, *A Traveller in Two
Worlds.* The third essay, "Politics," initially appeared in Dorothy Norman's New York omnibus *Twice-A-Year* in 1948 and was reprinted
in 1963 by Putnam's in Louis Filler's anthology of writing about the
1930's, *The Anxious Years.*

The first of the critical selections is the Introduction to my second book on Whitman. *Walt Whitman: The Critical Heritage* was com-
missioned and published in 1971 by Routledge and Kegan Paul in
London and by Barnes and Noble in New York.

The second selection served as the Introduction to a new edition
(in 1986) of the poet Charles Reznikoff's 1930 novel *By the Waters of
Manhattan,* published in New York by Markus Wiener.

The following essay is an Introduction to a 1985 edition of Whittaker Chambers's *Witness* published by Regnery-Gateway in Chicago.

This is followed by three essays on Irving Babbitt, the first published in *The University Bookman* in 1961. The second was an Introduction to a new edition of Babbitt's *Masters of Modern French Criticism*
published in 1963 by Farrar Straus in New York. The third was an
essay-review in *The New York Times Book Review* on March 28, 1965
of a New Directions edition of Babbitt's version of the Buddha's *Dhammapada* together with an essay on "Buddha and the Occident."

These three essays on Babbitt are followed by an essay on Socrates
vs. Thoreau on the subject of Civil Disobedience, which was published
in 1980 in *PN Review* in Manchester, England.

"The Pattern of Proustian Love" was published in *The University
of New Mexico Quarterly* in the Winter of 1951 and preceded my two
books on Proust: *The Proustian Vision* (New York, 1954) and *A Reader's
Guide to Proust* (New York, 1962).

"On Céline Once More" is an essay first published in 1983 in
a volume of *Brandeis Essays* edited by John Hazel Smith for the Brandeis
University Department of English.

Finally, "Reminiscences of Robert Frost" is an essay published
in 1979 by the magazine *Midstream* in New York.

Acknowledgments are made to the editors and publishers of the various books and periodicals in which these essays first appeared.

For substantial help in the publication of this book of selected essays, I am grateful first of all to the Marguerite Eyer Wilbur Foundation in Santa Barbara.

I'm also indebted to Brandeis University where these essays were written over the years and which has allowed me office-space since my retirement from the classroom there after thirty-three years.

Pieces out of
a Man's Life

The Tombstone

(a chapter of autobiography)

I call to the grave, Thou art my father.
The Book of Job, Chapter 17, verse 10

IT HAS BEEN SAID that the child is the meaning of life. Nietzsche
suggested that children constitute our true confessions. It is easy
to see the child as the future or the judgment of posterity. But such
statements can seem exaggerated when we reflect upon the remarkable
men in history—Socrates, the father of three, is a good example—
whose offspring have left no trace of themselves. And what of those
who had no children at all—like Beethoven? Marcus Aurelius counsels
us to take no stock in the verdict of posterity, and posterity has agreed
to separate Marcus Aurelius himself, the noblest and best of Roman
Emperors, from his son Commodus, one of the worst. And what again
of those, like Johann Sebastian Bach, whose numerous children (musi-
cians like their father) completely underestimated him and thought
themselves more endowed than he was?

The dispassionate world that passes judgment on us all, according to a well-known Latin maxim, does not confuse an individual's
just deserts with what his offspring, if any, are prepared to make of
them. A cynic has said that he who addresses himself to posterity
"declaims to an audience of maggots." And that, too, is true. There
is no guaranty that the judgment made by the child will be true, only
that, in most cases, where it is not overborne and corrected by a world
of others, it is likely to be the only one. The unanswerable argument
will be that of the survivor.

How can one explain to one's child everything that has happened
to make one go wrong in life, everything of which the ignorant
child is likely to be intolerant? Each little child is a perfectionist
who despises excuses and wants to know nothing of alibis. The world
lies around him in a vast circle of doors opening on the infinite, and
though, in time, these doors begin to close one by one and the infinite

15

perspectives to recede and shrink more and more to the here and now, this does not serve to make the child any more tolerant of those who have begotten him. On the contrary, if I may judge by my own feelings of long ago, it may make him more resentful of his parents. There they are, the very ones responsible for his existence and all his problems and sufferings. Shouldn't they have known better? Had life been so great in their own experience that they had not hesitated to pass it on to another unfortunate biped? Perhaps only those without imagination or memory will not recognize such thoughts and feelings as their own at some point in their pilgrimage through "this vale of tears," especially in their early years or the more difficult passages in their adolescence.

After many years of neglect, I went to the cemetery to visit my father's grave, and I found myself in a state of confusion there. I had had difficulty crying at his funeral, and I experienced the same difficulty again here, though I had come in a spirit of contrition. An aunt of mine had shamed me into making the visit, but once I was there I was filled with peculiar and contradictory thoughts. I had never seen the tombstone that had been erected with part of the insurance money, which he had made over to his brothers, who had shouldered the considerable financial burden after he had been stricken by cancer. That insurance, at the time, might have helped me up one important step in the economic struggle for existence. His brothers had clearly not stinted in their expense upon that tall white stone with the star of David engraved upon it. It was the biggest and finest one in that part of the cemetery, and I could not help thinking how pleased he would have been with it. What other criterion is there for judging what is right in such situations? In the presence of the dead themselves, my Platonism made me think of everything as if there is no death (as Whitman assures us) and both the living and the dead buried here were part of an endless stream of eternal life. Grant for a moment that the dead may be aware of what is happening here, and we cannot help feeling that we must continue to act as they would have wished us to when they were alive. At the same time, we cannot help being in some doubt about this; even Socrates grants at one point that his postulate about immortality may be mistaken and that death may indeed be, as it appears to be, an endless sleep and loss of consciousness. That's what I mean about being filled with even more contradictions than usual here on the cemetery.

I knew that the most important feeling in my father's life had been that of the inferiority he had to labor under, as a poor man especially in comparison with his brothers who had come to this country later than he did but had prospered much more and become financially successful in a short time. This feeling of inferiority might have been appeased somewhat by the prominence of this stone. My uncles were therefore right in spending as much as they did upon it. But I could not help reflecting at the same time on the wasted years it had cost me. It was the lack of money that had interrupted my professional education and therefore postponed for a long time the achievement of security that the completion of these studies would have given me. Suddenly I realized that the proud white stone rested not only on my father's grave but on my own life as well. And I almost gave way to tears of self-pity instead of crying for my father as I felt I ought to have done.

I did not really feel any resentment because of these thoughts, only a vague sort of curiosity and wonder, because I could hardly be sure that a father really owes any help to his son if it means depriving himself of a tombstone taller than those of his neighbors. Besides, the decision about the stone had been made not by my father himself but by his brothers, who no doubt resented the fact that the burden of his final illness had fallen upon themselves instead of upon me where it belonged in their opinion. Wasn't I of an age to bear it? But I was as unsuccessful in worldly terms as my father had been, and some of these Americanized uncles of mine (not all of them, by any means, as I shall indicate later on), who let themselves be influenced too much by money, had little respect for either of us. The only time I really saw them moved at his funeral was when the Rabbi mentioned the fact that my father had been the pioneer in the family and that he had been responsible for bringing them over to this land, which they seemed to have understood much better than he did.

But suppose I had been given some of the insurance money at the time and been able to finish my education and had things made easier for me at that time, would I have reimbursed them for the cost of this impressive stone? The answer is that, though I don't like to think of myself as sentimental, I really am at bottom, and I have always paid off my debts even when I could ill-afford to do so. But, of course, one can't be absolutely sure, and how were my uncles, who didn't really know me very well at the time, supposed to read my character? Now that I actually saw the stone, I wondered if a more modest or less ostentatious one might not have served as well. After all, it was not as if he were being consigned to a nameless grave in Potter's field for the indigent. So I stood there with dry eyes, thoughtfully considering the unfathomable mystery of life, as I was so often inclined to do.

I asked one of the old men, who always seem to be around somewhere on Jewish cemeteries expecting alms from visitors and mourners to say a prayer for my father's soul. He asked me about my mother, since he wished to mention her, too, in his prayer, but his question disturbed me, because it opened for me a whole painful family history which I did not feel like going into. I tried to ignore his question, but he looked at me so fixedly I felt that I had to tell him that, though she was still living, they had been estranged from each other at the time of his death and therefore that he was to say his prayer only on my own behalf. When he had finished reciting the Hebrew text, which I thought he did with feeling for his vocation, humble as it was, I gave him the alms he expected, and he walked away and left me to my thoughts. He seemed to me a cheerful old man, taking pleasure in his own vigorous life among the graves. It was clear from the inscriptions that many of those interred here had been brought to their final resting place at an age much younger than he was now.

After the old man left, I wandered around the area of my father's grave, kicking at the gravel occasionally and looking down at the ground with an uncomfortable conscience, because I could still not summon up any tears for him, despite all the sadness thinking of him made me feel. If only there had been someone with me as there had been at his funeral, my social nature if not my moral feelings may have been touched to the point of shedding at least some token tears for him, but as it was, there was only an indescribable feeling of emptiness and nothingness within me. And even this seemed to be saying too much. I looked up at the trees and watched the wind blow through the leaves and branches with a noise that sounded incongruously like castanets. I wondered in what seemed like an ostentatious literary way if it were not spirit that was moving them, if the wind were not but another name for spirit. I knew, of course, that the word spirit was related somehow to the breath of life, to fire, and that in some religions it was a synonym for God Himself . . . Weeds had begun to spring up around my father's grave, because my uncles had stopped with the tombstone and left the upkeep otherwise to me. Until this time, it was only too evident that I had done nothing.

Finally, instead of crying, I made a speech to my father's grave. I apologized to God for having behaved for years as if I were so indifferent to his existence that I had not troubled even to doubt it. I reminded myself unfortunately of that cynical agnostic I had known who had speculated that he himself might be something of a god to the tiny submicroscopic creatures who inhabited his body, living or dead. In other words, I resembled an arrogant creature who worshipped at his own shrine unlike Socrates, who has sometimes been called an agnostic and who had no absolute assurance of anything but yet managed to humble himself before his Maker and was prepared to make the necessary leap of faith in his existence and power. I said aloud: "I certainly feel humble at this moment, and I ask you, God, if you have a place reserved for suffering souls like my father, be kind to him, as no one here on earth was ever kind to him. Dear father, if you can hear me, I want you to know that your son has not forgotten you."

I felt terribly embarrassed all this time, even though no one could hear me. I was embarrassed before that part of myself, perhaps more than half, which was modern and "scientific" rather than superstitious in an old-fashioned way. I seemed, on this cemetery, to have reverted somehow to my childhood when I listened open-mouthed and trembling to my immigrant grandmother telling ghost stories from "the old country." She may not have been filled with religious convictions like my grandfather, but she was much more superstitious. Superstition is the shadowy side of the medal of religion, and it was this that had communicated itself to me. Despite these misgivings, however, my "address" to the silent grave affected me very much. It made me feel that, regardless of what might be true of any other world (such as that which my grandparents believed in), my father was very much alive and actively functioning still in this world, through myself, and that he would go on doing so, as long as I lived. This sounds, I'm afraid, trite and undistinguished as a thought, yet it somehow gripped me suddenly with such emotional power that it ended by making me feel tears start to my eyes, though almost immediately I was aware of how awkward and silly it might all seem to an observer, had any been present. My tears "froze"; they were at once dammed up. In the eighteenth century the "man of feeling" was admired and the capacity for tears could be one for a sentimental man to boast of in his Confessions. But I was a hard-hearted man of my own time. The whole performance I was putting on before myself for my own benefit really disgusted me. I was both actor and audience, and hardly a sympathetic one.

I walked away from the grave and sat down on a little rusty iron bench considerately put there for visitors. Self-consciously I spread out the newspaper which I had brought along but had carefully put away till now. But the news of the day, I found, appeared to me in a much different light. I suddenly doubted the importance of what I had been inclined to accept uncritically. I almost felt like throwing the newspaper away. I began to understand better those of my friends who were not newspaper readers at all, because, as one of them put it, he was allergic to the smell of fresh print, which often came off the page and blackened your hand. I was prepared more than ever to understand the abyss that separates "the news that is fit to print" because it is startling in the man-bites-dog sense and the "news that stays news" which is literature and is so quiet and unobtrusive and ordinary that it may never be recognized by a journalist at all. What I was feeling on this cemetery was certainly news, but how was one to tell anyone else about it unless he was prepared to be patient and attentive to subtleties and shadings which would be wasted upon the unprepared?

But this perception of mine lasted only a short time. As I continued to read the paper, there seemed less and less difference between reading on the cemetery and reading anywhere else. I ceased being philosophically detached and grew more interested in the usual trivia and involved with worldly stories, values, and affairs. The change and contrast between the two attitudes were so great that suddenly I found myself laughing without being really amused, and I had to get up and go back to look once more at my father's grave. Since there were still no tears, I decided to examine some of the other monuments and read their histories and inscriptions. The part of the cemetery where my father was buried belonged to The Progressive Workingmen's Association, a benevolent mutual-aid society of a type common among Jewish immigrants. Their principal functions were to help as much as they could in times of dire or catastrophic need and, even more importantly, to bury their deceased members and their families decently. There may be people in the world who would not give priority to such needs, but immigrant Jews were not among them. The culture was hardly an irresponsible one. It was a family-oriented, responsibly social, and basically believing world, even when the religious tie to the synagogue, as in my father's case, had worn somewhat thin. The workers in the humblest trades and employments in America have long aspired to put aside a little "burial money," and the possible lack of it haunted the imaginations of newly-arrived Jews in a strange land where everybody was expected to take care of and be responsible for himself. The mutual-aid societies thus allayed some real fears and anxieties.

I noted that all the men were buried on one side and all the women on the other. It seemed as if the sexes were not to mingle either in the Orthodox synagogue or on this cemetery, though most of the members of this association were hardly Orthodox, so it could not have been religious scruples that explained the division. It must have been something Puritanical in immigrant Jewish life itself that was responsible.

The graves were packed tightly together in this section, because those buried here had limited means, and land in New York, even on cemeteries in what had once been (and in many cases still are) outlying sections of the city, was expensive. There were other sections of the cemetery, which I explored, where the more wealthy were buried, and not only did they have more space (there was no crowding there of one grave hard upon another), but some were interred in impressive stone tombs, with family names carved large in granite and lovely blue panes of glass in the windows of the front doors. Even on this cemetery, class distinctions of the kind familiar elsewhere were strictly preserved. Vanity, not surprisingly, followed one into eternity as much as it ever did among the ancients. Someone had spoken of "the great democracy of the dead," but there was little sign of equality here. I confess to a feeling of embarrassment for the poor, exposed as they were to all weathers, and crowded together as they had once been at the rush-hour, going to and from work. The deity who created this world seemed to have liked his handiwork so much that he preserved its essential patterns in death as in life.

I examined some of the other graves and tombstones carefully. Since this section belonged to my father's association and they were all members of it, I was not surprised to recognize the names. Some were those of distant relatives, and some were my father's cronies who came to the house sometimes on Sunday afternoons to play pinochle or poker with him. There was another odd thing I found. Many of the tombstones had small photographs of the occupants of the graves on them. These were often flattering, and they were surprisingly young. Examination of the dates of birth and death recorded on the stones indicated clearly that life expectancy among the immigrants was not high, and considering their occupations and the conditions in which they lived, this was scarcely surprising. Incongruously, what these little pictures brought to mind was something I had read about the cemetery where Proust's parents were buried and how his mother had been anxious, after her husband's death, to have a very handsome photograph of him put on the tombstone. The practice was something that the immigrants must have brought with them from Europe, and frankly I thought it in terrible taste. But it had a weird effect on my imagination to look at the picture of a youthful face and consider what must be the state of it now. There was no thought of cremation then among immigrant Jews.

There were pebbles and little stones placed carefully atop some of the monuments by previous visitors in a kind of silent communication to later ones. The old man had informed me that such was the custom on Jewish cemeteries, and I remembered Proust making a similar observation when he described visiting the graveyard where his mother's Jewish relatives were buried. Proust's father was Catholic, and he himself was baptized at birth and was buried by the church when he died, but he never lost his feeling of piety towards his mother's ancestors, since she herself had never adopted her husband's faith "out of respect for her parents" and he felt closer to her than to his father and has been treated by some therefore as spiritually Jewish. I don't think he himself would have appreciated that. The custom is very likely a pagan survival of the kind which, among the Celts, produced the cairn of small stones to which each successive visitor and passerby was expected to contribute and which was meant to mark the place where some eminent chieftain had been buried. Though I was only too keenly aware that my father had been neither eminent nor a chieftain, I picked up a stone from the ground and placed it reverently on his tombstone.

After this, I continued for a long time to visit the cemetery regularly. In fact, I went there more often than custom strictly required. I found that, instead of depressing me (as I had feared in the years I had stayed away after my father's death), going there somehow helped to restore me to myself. It would be going too far to call it enjoyable (and possibly suggest some nasty perversion), but I found a keener awareness of many things while I was there. The cemetery seemed to open a whole new range of experience to me. In the presence of this burial place of the dead, I began to feel more alive. I enjoyed an awareness of the simplest things of nature as I had never done before. The trees and sky had never seemed quite so wonderful elsewhere. The dead paradoxically seemed to be living in the country year-round, without any worries or responsibilities. These thoughts seemed odd and somewhat literary and suspect even to me, and they were undoubtedly the expression of a deepseated pessimism. But I'm telling how it felt to me without second-guessing. Every bird that flew, every leaf that stirred seemed to me a victory of life, a fragment broken off from death. The cemetery seemed anything but sad to me. In fact, it seemed so pleasant I was happy that no one else had discovered it as yet. But, of course, most people put off going till it's absolutely necessary, and then their perspective is necessarily distorted. They don't see the cemetery as I saw it. They don't feel the sense of detachment and superiority it gives you to all the important events and doings and politics of the world.

I even eventually realized my wish to be able to cry at my father's grave. It happened the day my mother came with me to the cemetery and it was unexpected and caught us both completely by surprise. Though I had long hoped for these tears of expiation and they certainly came as a relief, I had not thought they would flow with such abundance and ease. After entering the cemetery, my mother and I had taken a winding path to the section where my father was buried, and on the way we passed a burial party led by a Rabbi who was chanting the service for the dead while the mourners stood around, looking uneasy, I thought. We walked by them, talking lightly of one thing or another until we actually came in sight of my father's grave and then the mere sight of the tombstone unleashed such cries and sobs within me as I had not thought possible. I'm not actually sure if it was not my mother who first broke into tears, but in any case it was her presence that was the catalyst that produced my own reaction, for there was no difference between my first visit to the cemetery and this one except for the fact that she was with me.

This was her own first visit in the seven years since he died. She had not even attended his funeral, because I had asked her not to. They had not been living together at the time of his death, and they had been separated from each other a number of times over the years. In fact, it had not been a good marriage, though it had never been formally broken off and there were periodic and half-hearted reconciliations, undertaken in part for my benefit and because they didn't seem to know what else to do. At the time of his death, I had been afraid that some coarse-grained member of his family (which blamed my mother and her family for the couple's difficulties) might take advantage of the social occasion of his funeral (always a particularly difficult occasion among the immigrants, because the customs of expressing one's grief in the old country differed so widely from those of the new one) and say something reproachful, hurtful or even insulting to her. I had wanted to spare both her and myself the ordeal. Besides, I was young enough then to be all in favor of sincerity and against hypocrisy of any kind, even that which in later life may seem not only excusable but praiseworthy. It was I who visited him in the hospital and nursing-home during the final days of his heartbreaking struggle against cancer. Afterwards, I began to doubt if I had really done the right or wise thing in encouraging her to stay away from the funeral. It may have helped to heal the family rift instead of widening it. But it was too late to do anything.

As the years passed, I was unable to find any rest until I had somehow managed to make peace between them, even if it had to be done beyond the grave. Why this should have been so, I could not have said. I didn't really know. Though I had tried to spare her suffering at the funeral, I realized that visiting his grave on the cemetery with me would also be a painful trial to her. Nevertheless, here she was with me, and since, as she had grown old, tears increasingly rose up in her for any reason at all and sometimes for no reason, it is small wonder that on such a provocative occasion as this, she should break into tears. Tears, as I have said, are rare with me and come only very hard, but perhaps it was her presence and example that released my grief as it had not been released before.

On that day, like myself on an earlier occasion, my mother was also moved to make a speech to the dead. I was not prepared for it, but it went, as nearly as I can remember, something like this: "My husband, forgive me! I cannot go on living without your forgiveness. I wronged you I know. But our failure was not really the fault of either of us. Circumstances were against us. Those circumstances against which you continually complained. It's not right, I know, to blame other people for what happens to us. But really it was not our fault. We were two gentle people, perhaps too gentle. Others were able to impose their will upon us . . . Now you must rest well, as I myself shall also rest soon. We are going to meet again somewhere in a better world . . . Forgive me!"

What my mother said made sense only to someone who had lived in our house, with my grandmother and grandfather, two brothers of my mother, my father and myself. My mother was hardly an intellectual woman with a complicated mind and complex feelings. It must have taken a tremendous effort for her to make this analysis and confession. She must have thought a long time and struggled mightily with her own contradictory feelings and multiple loyalties to have achieved it. But it was a catharsis for herself and for me too. I confess that I was profoundly moved. At that moment, and even for a long time afterwards, I had to accept what she had said as completely true.

−1941

Portrait of an Uncle

"IF YOU WANT TO WRITE," my uncle Maurice Hindus used to say to me, "why don't you leave the city and go to work on a farm?"

I discovered later on that I was not the only one of his nephews to whom he had given similar advice to leave home and explore the real America that was to be found outside New York City, according to him, and especially among those people who worked on the land. I didn't know, until I had read his memoirs, how much little places like North Brookfield in upstate New York had meant to him. He had gone to work there as an immigrant boy of seventeen, hardly three years in this country, for a farmer named Jim Moore, who had advertised for hired help through an employment agency on the Lower East Side. Moore had eventually become almost a second father to him, and the autobiographical *Green Worlds* is dedicated to his memory: "the most irascible friend, the most sensible teacher, the most humane Americanizer I have ever known."

Like much well-meant advice from older people to younger ones, his to me, I'm afraid, fell on deaf ears. It didn't seem very pertinent to me. It was too simple for my taste and reflected, I thought, the somewhat smug attitude of a self-made man who was inclined to make a fetish out of the particular experience that had brought him success and to believe that the road which had led him to a certain goal was the only road there was to it. To connect working on a farm with the art of writing seemed a ridiculous *non sequitur* to me, for I realized even then, from a careful reading of Proust, that the material which a writer used counted for much less than the treatment which he was able to give it. Writing was "creative" precisely in the degree that it was able to perform the seemingly impossible feat of making a silk purse out of a sow's ear. Flaubert had even proposed to rival the Deity by writing a great book about *nothing at all*.

The surroundings in which my uncle's advice was given added to its incongruity. My conversations with him usually took place in the living-working room of his duplex apartment in the solid old Hotel des Artistes west of Central Park. The ceiling of this room, two stories high, with a huge wrought iron chandelier, the windows twenty feet or more in height, the bareness of much of the wall space above the low-slung bookcases lining the room on all sides with volumes in Russian, English, and other languages — all the space and filtered light gave to the studio the air of a chapel in a cathedral. There was a mixture there of elegance and asceticism, and the presence in one corner of a small desk with a typewriter on it, manuscript pages scattered about, and the portion of the heavy carpet near the desk most worn out plainly hinted that the room was more used by a working writer than it was for entertaining. The boy who had once astonished his high school principal by telling him that his ambition was to become a farmer and had subsequently actually become one before he had become an educated man and a writer had obviously gone very far, in my view, from the pastoral life to which he seemed to be seeking, as if by proxy, to return through me. I did not know, then, that no matter how far-flung his travels, he continued to return to the country around North Brookfield, where he had so many friends and memories, very nearly to the last day of his life.

How little we know and understand each other, or manage, across the vast distances and abysses that separate even members of the same family from each other, to communicate, and that little, more often than not, by chance or indirection. On one of the walls of my uncle's apartment there was a juxtaposition or balancing of two beautiful, framed photographs that may or may not have been symbolic. They were both studies of bearded old men's heads. One was of George Bernard Shaw, inscribed by him to my uncle, in gratitude as I later learned for his having acted, soon after having become famous as an interpreter of Russia to the West, as Shaw's "guide, philosopher and friend" during a trip to Russia in the 1930s. Shaw's brow in this picture is massively intellectual and his aged face of a man in his middle seventies is unmistakably individualistic and brightly observant in expression. Yet the other picture is no less impressive. The head is positively Tolstoyan in its weight and dignity, but it is a picture of an anonymous Russian taken by Margaret Bourke-White during a visit to some remote Russian village.

I wondered if Maurice was trying to say something by balancing off the world-famous celebrity against the nameless Russian. It seemed to me that if any single idea informed the score of books he wrote during his life, it was that the common man, especially if he were one who worked on the land, was filled with spiritual and intellectual riches equaling if not exceeding those possessed by the more prominent and well-to-do who were so often empty—what Whitman liked to call "damned simulacra," stuffed shirts devoid of real inner worth and substance. This Wordsworthian or romantic notion transpires through his most touching and tender pages, which, though they are written in prose, are transfigured by a poetic quality in the descriptions of landscape and the simpler joys of rustic life. The pictures were emblematic of the two sides of his life. He had consorted with people like Shaw, Lady Astor, Lord Lothian, Wendell Willkie, Jan Masaryk, F. Scott Fitzgerald, Clarence Darrow, William Jennings Bryan, and Helen Keller without being spoiled for the enjoyment of the company of the humble dirt farmers who had been his friends and employers in upstate New York or the unlettered muzhiks of the Russian countryside in which he had been born. If a choice had had to be made, he might even have felt more at home with the latter than in the exciting and colorful intellectual and social world that his talents had opened to him.

Maurice was born in the small Byelorussian village of Bolshoye Bykovo in 1891, a member of one of the four Jewish families in the village. It was located in the Pale of Settlement to which most Russian Jews were confined by the Czar. The law prevented people of Jewish faith from owning land, but his grandfather, who was something of a favorite of the well-known Polish Count Radziwill, the largest landowner of the vicinity, was able to rent a large acreage from the nobleman. Maurice used to recall that his own father, in the days of his greatest prosperity, owned ten horses, twenty cows, many calves, geese, and hens, as well as the only horse-drawn threshing machine, "the sole mark of the machine age in the community." Unfortunately, his father, though very kind, proved quite improvident, produced too many offspring even for his ample resources (no less than seventeen, by two wives), was a poor businessman, showed a quite uncharacteristic love of vodka in his later years, and, at his death, left an impoverished family—a widow and numerous children.

My father, who was the oldest of eleven children of my grandfather's second marriage, came to the United States around the turn of the century. He entered the women's clothing industry, like Abraham Cahan's character David Levinsky, but unlike that tycoon he prospered only very indifferently. By 1905, however, he was sufficiently established to help his mother and some of his younger brothers and sisters, among them Maurice, to emigrate. The need to do so was dire. 1905 was the year of the first of three major Russian revolutions in this century. It was an unforgettable year for anyone who managed to survive it. Unexpected defeat at the hands of tiny Japan rocked the Czar's empire to its foundations. The first Soviet, with the twenty-eight-year old revolutionary Leon Trotsky conspicuous among its leaders, spontaneously sprang into existence. Backlash and reaction against the revolutionaries took the form of peasant pogroms against the Jews.

The village of Bolshoye Bykovo itself was spared the horrors and atrocities that occurred elsewhere in Russia, perhaps because the number of Jews was so small and their relations with the Orthodox priest of the village very amicable. There were no tales of terror among my father's people to match those of my mother's family which had come over to this country in the same fateful year. News of the social explosions in St. Petersburg and the repercussions they had provoked spread widely, of course, and all Jews were happy to find refuge in the United States, but there was no feeling, as my uncle told the story, of the kind recorded by Mary Antin in her *Promised Land* of being liberated and going from darkness into light. On the contrary, he never forgot his experience of what he called "the desolation of the uprooted." With all its faults, he had formed deep attachments to the country in which he had been born and to its people, and leaving them was "like tearing something out" of his very soul.

His memories of the fields, forests, and streams among which he had spent his childhood and boyhood became all the more tormenting when they were contrasted with the realities of the East Side ghetto to which he came — its overcrowded tenements, sweatshops, pushcarts, peddlers, mountainous piles of garbage, vermin, and the other signs and stigmata of urban poverty. Cooped up in a small airless bedroom with two older brothers, he soon began to dream of leaving the hellish city behind him and making his way into the interior of the country in search of a counterpart of the village he remembered. He grew literally sick of Manhattan, developed a heart murmur, a touch of tuberculosis, and began making endless dreary pilgrimages to clinics in search of the elusive state of health that neither medicines nor pills produced. Only the atmosphere that he found on Jim Moore's farm restored him, and to the end of his days, when "the world was too much with him," he claimed that, more effective than a visit to the doctor or psychiatrist, was going up to the country where he had spent his youth and helping one of his farmer friends with his chores. The prescription seemed to work for him, too. No wonder he came to think it a cure-all for everything that ever troubled anyone.

In making a name for himself eventually as a writer on Russia, war correspondent, and lecturer on public platforms throughout the country and over nationwide radio, he also gave a feeling of identity, of belonging to America, and even of pride to those of us who were related to him. It was only reflected glory, to be sure, but that may be better than nothing at all. It impressed me, for example, when I first entered college to find that my family name was recognized by more than one of my professors, who asked if I were related to him and seemed to expect something more of me because I was. Mary McCarthy observes in *The Company She Keeps* that "if you scratch a Socialist, you find a snob." The truth seems to be that if you scratch almost anyone at random you find a streak of snobbishness underneath. All of us are in need of support for our desire to be slightly special and superior in some respect, and the accomplishments of my uncle Maurice were, for a long time, the source which fed this conviction in our family.

Because this was so, it's easy to understand the feelings of excitement he inspired when he appeared at a family gathering, such as a wedding or bar mitzvah. Whispers would quickly run around the room, especially among the more impressionable youngsters: "Maurice Hindus is here!"

In family photographs on such occasions, he was always given a central place even if his relation to the event was very peripheral, but in any case, the distinction of his features, the unruliness of his hair, and the unusual brightness of his eyes (which occasionally gave him a surprised and even startled look) would have been sufficient to make his face stand out among the others in any picture. He was pleased by such attentions, less because of vanity, I think, than because, like many childless men (though married), he was intensely family-minded and had something that can only be called an avuncular vocation, which made him take an interest in his many nephews and nieces and eventually even in their children. A large number of people in the family can remember receiving from him, at one time or another, completely unexpected gifts or missives evincing his kindness and concern for them.

After he had become markedly successful, everyone in the family treated him as an "elder statesman" whose advice was sought on all sorts of subjects. Even those who were chronologically older deferred to him with "the deep almost worshiping respect enjoined by an inferior order of endowment toward a higher." But it had not always been so. There were family legends, later confirmed by himself, that his brothers had regarded his passion for reading with scant sympathy when he kept the light on late at night and interfered with the sleep they sorely needed in order to go out in the morning to work a twelve-hour day. In his memoirs he recalls having to prepare his lessons for school in the bathroom because of this. An older sister, who had married a quite affluent man, had refused at one point to lend him a mere fifty dollars which he desperately needed to pay for his tuition at Colgate University. Even after he had finished college, attended the Harvard Graduate School, and published his first book, *The Russian Peasant and the Revolution,* in 1920, but before there was any large public recognition of his talents, he was still known among the family in Brownsville as *der meshugenneh philosophe* (Yiddish, roughly meaning "the crazy philosopher").

My own memories of him go back to my childhood, but his visits to our apartment I remember less directly than indirectly through the recollection of the complaints of my poor mother, who was meticulously neat and orderly as a housewife, concerning the watery mess he had made of her whole bathroom while taking a shower. Also, I seem to recollect his sleeping out on the fire escape of the apartment house in which we lived, which caused some comment. He may have acquired this habit while living on the East Side where sleeping on the fire escape or the roof was a recognized way of escaping the stifling heat of the tenements during the summer. Or else it may have been due to the health and fresh-air fads he had imbibed from the writings of Bernarr MacFadden. He had also spent some time, as I later learned, among the pacifist and vegetarian sects of Russian Doukhobor peasants who had settled in Western Canada and would occasionally annoy the government authorities by marching in the nude upon Ottawa to express their indignation about some measure. He had written his earliest articles about these schismatics for Glenn Frank's old *Century Magazine,* and he had obviously been imbued with the utmost sympathy for the naïveté of their ideas and the eccentricities of their behavior. These unlettered peasants had somehow arrived at conclusions strangely similar to those of Tolstoy whom they had never read, or perhaps it was the other way about and he had reached conclusions similar to theirs. Both their way of life and way of thought were fascinating to Maurice, and he made his magazine reports of them so interesting that the editor was inspired to commission him to go back to his native Russian village in 1923 to do a series of articles reporting on the changes which the Revolution had made in peasant life as he remembered it. It was out of this assignment that his book *Broken Earth* came in 1926.

But at the outset, the family regarded Maurice himself as an eccentric. He was the only one who had left the city to go back to work on the land, though eventually he managed to get for himself a formal education that was unique in its extent and thoroughness among the immigrant generation of the Hinduses. His choice of the risky vocations of writer and lecturer also made his family suspect his soundness until there was hard evidence that it had worked out successfully despite the odds against him. As happens so often, public recognition preceded private recognition by those closest to him.

My own more certain memories of him begin about the time I entered college as a freshman and promptly fell, as if through a trap door, into one of the extreme student movements, which were as popular among us in the 1930s as, after a long period in the shadows, they are once more coming to be. My father, a reader of Cahan's Yiddish paper, the *Jewish Daily Forward,* was a mild Socialist in theory and a voting Democrat in practice, and he was alarmed at my turn toward radicalism and revolution. He took me, therefore, to see my uncle Maurice, hoping that the latter might help to moderate my views somewhat. And that is what he did in the end, not by any direct onslaught against my theories, but by counteracting my utopian view of Russia with a dose of realism. He could appreciate the fact that my ideological development had not been entirely gratuitous. There were real grievances, like the Depression, which had struck serious blows against my family and me, and I was attempting to respond to these grievances. He was not one of those who forget the enthusiasms of their youth completely. He, too, had felt the sting of social injustice and had been thrilled by his discovery as an immigrant of the various peddlers of panaceas designed to perfect the world. In his autobiography he tells how on East Broadway were to be found "Anarchists, Social Revolutionaries, Social Democrats, Populists, Zionists, Zangwillites, Assimilationists, Internationalists, Single Taxers, Republicans, Democrats, each group with its own gods, dead and alive, its own demons too . . ." The trouble was that, as he listened to them, he discovered that "the prophets of the various causes and their disciples were not wise or strong enough so to fortify their ideological positions that opponents couldn't demolish them." And so, after much reflection, he had "decided that [he] was neither clever enough nor old and experienced enough to be a crusader for any abstract ideal."

There was no way to transmit this conclusion to me directly, yet he must have made me feel that there was a quality of *déjà vu,* so far as he was concerned, about theories that seemed to me then novel and exciting. We also talked of Russia, of course, and he brought to my attention the fact that while capitalist America was in the grip of a great economic depression, which was the immediate source of

my own unhappiness and desire for sweeping change in the system,
"Communist" Russia, to which we all looked then as an example of
what a well-planned, orderly, and idealistic society should be, was
in the grip of a famine that was destroying millions of peasants in
the Ukraine, and that this famine was not really necessary, but had
been produced by the brutal, pigheaded, doctrinaire policies of the
Soviet government. Now it must be realized that at the time, a
strenuous effort was being made by Communists and their fellow-
travelers to deny the very existence of this famine. It seemed to us
that only political reactionaries and the Hearst yellow tabloid press
would spread such slanderous stories. I was dumfounded to hear them
from the lips of my uncle, who was a liberal and progressive and
recognized many positive achievements of the Revolution. Such was
my impassioned intolerance and fanaticism at that moment in my
youth that, for a flickering instant, I lumped my uncle together in
my mind with Hearst and the right-wing reactionaries. Yet it was
impossible for me to maintain this attitude for very long. Our family
ties and his patent honesty of purpose prevented me from dismissing
what he told me with the same ease with which I dismissed other facts
that accorded uncomfortably with my radical theories.

Nor could I readily refute or discount the cogent analysis by which
he sought to demonstrate to me that, in defiance of Marxist analysis,
the Russian Revolution was a phenomenon that grew out of the
specifics of Russian history and more particularly out of the age-old
peasant hunger for land, which had caused revolts of a magnitude
that had shaken the Czar's throne long before Marxism was even
known in Russia. He pooh-poohed the idea that the Russian Revolution was a harbinger of world revolution. It was hardly an accident,
he said, that, despite all of the fantasies and wish-fulfillments and activity of Lenin and Trotsky, the Russian Revolution had died on the
Russian frontier. It was most improbable that a violent overturn along
similar lines would ever occur in any of the industrialized nations of
the western world, and the possibility was especially remote in such
a society as that of the United States. In countries that had a land
problem analogous to Russia's, such as China and those in southeast
Asia, however, it was not impossible that the Russian example might
prove powerful, but that was certainly not because of Marxist theory.
Such observations seemed very farfetched to me then, because they
ran counter to all of my romantic notions, but, in retrospect, it appears to me that he did much in a quiet and unostentatious way to
restore me to a more balanced and sounder outlook on the world than
was fashionable among those of my contemporaries who shared my

views. It was only much later that I learned from him what good company I had unwittingly been in at that time. Just about the period
when my father had brought me to him in order to have him dampen
some of my illusions about the Soviets, F. Scott Fitzgerald had sought
him out in order to have him allay his fears that a violent Communist
revolution might well be imminent in the United States. The substance
of what he said to both of us, for those who are curious, may be found
in the last chapter, entitled "The Collapse of World Revolution," of
a book he published in 1933 called *The Great Offensive*.

He influenced me because he was never heavy-handed in his approach. More quickly than my parents he grasped the fact that I insisted more stubbornly than most upon finding or making my own
path in life and that all attempts to force an issue with me were more
likely than not to prove, as the jargon nowadays has it, "counterproduc-
tive." When he found that I did not resemble him in his attachment
to the land or his romantic idealization of a rural life but that I still
insisted on becoming a writer on my own terms, he did what he could
for me. He helped me financially, he let me use his apartment for
long periods of time while he was traveling abroad, he read everything
I wrote, and gave me promptly his impressions of it. He did not flatter
and he tried to be objective. In my younger days, he was more critical
of what I did than later on, without ever being discouraging. Eventually he came to view my work with the kindness of a kinsman and
not at all with the envy of a rival or competitor engaged in the same
line of work. Such an attitude is not too usual, in my experience, even
among writers who are very friendly or related to each other. It sprang
in his case from a generosity that was fundamental to his character.

It may be best perhaps to conclude with an assessment of him
by a man of his own generation, whose vision is unclouded by the
partiality of a relation and who is inclined to express himself with
restraint rather than overstatement. Here is what Louis Fischer says
in his book *Men and Politics*: "Maurice Hindus came frequently to
Moscow and wrote some excellent books. He could never bear Moscow
for more than a week or so, and soon he would sling his shoes over
his shoulder like the Russian peasant — the peasant did it to save his
shoes but Maurice to save his feet — and tour the countryside. He is
simple and loves simple people. He is a farmer and loves the soil.
Hindus has a tremendous capacity for warmth and affection. He par-
ticipates in the suffering and joys of others; and he frequently emp-
ties his purse to friends. He was born in a Russian village and appreciated what the Bolsheviks were doing to lift the villages out of
the Czarist mire. Doubts frequently tormented him, as they did all

of us, but when they tormented him he was disconsolate and grim
and yearned either for frivolity or, more frequently, for a soul-interview
with a kindred spirit . . . He understands emotions and ignores
economics. He despised Communist terminology and Marxist logic,
and admired the Soviets only for what they did to uproot and give
new life to humanity. Hindus is humble, and honestly avows his limitations, accepting assistance when he needs it. He is an American lecture audience's ideal: dramatic, passionate, personal, romantic-looking,
and not too high-brow."

But I would add that there are some things in this description
that I myself should change. If Maurice was something of a muzhik,
he was also a muzhik with a difference; if he was simple, he was, like
that peasant who posed for the photograph by Margaret Bourke-White
that now hangs on my own living-room wall, also profound. But the
general outlines of Fischer's sketch are certainly recognizable to me
and to all who knew him. While I was driving down to New York
in July 1969 to attend his funeral and reflected on the obituaries that
had come not only from various parts of the country but from Europe,
I suddenly recalled something that Emerson had said to Whitman on
Boston Common in 1860 to buoy up his self-confidence: "You have
put the world in your debt, and such obligations are always
acknowledged and met." It may be that these words are applicable,
in a measure, to all those who, like my uncle Maurice, are blessed
with the capacity to give to others more than they have ever received
from others themselves.

— 1971

Politics
A chapter from
The Confessions of a Young Man

IN HIGH SCHOOL, as anyone will say who knew me at that time, I kept very quiet. Persons who met me later in my revolutionary days and remembered me as a shy boy could not reconcile the two. But there was a simple explanation. I didn't change. These people should have seen me during my elementary school days when I was called "the question box" by some of my teachers who could not keep up with my insatiable curiosity. In high school I was under wraps, so to speak, because of an incident in the last year of elementary school which shattered my confidence for a long time to come.

It happened in this way. History had always been my best subject. That was so because from the moment I began to read, I continually kept reading books of history. We had only a few books in the house, because we were not an intellectual family. We did have two books, however, which I was always reading. One was Montgomery's *American History* — an advanced textbook and certainly difficult reading for a boy of eight. The other book was *A Nemesis of Misgovernment* — a heavy book which dealt with Russia under the Czars. It had a dull green cover which I clearly remember, though it was by an author whose name I don't remember.

What I got out of these books was not what the authors intended me to get out of them. To me both books were filled with adventure and romance. Simply to look at them was enough to start me dreaming. I was buried in them at every spare moment, and I read them over and over again. If I didn't understand the intricacies of a legislative argument as it was explained by Montgomery, the fact of conflict I certainly did apprehend, and I absorbed enough technical information with my enjoyment to last me well into my college years. Most of my knowledge proved beyond the range of my first teachers, and this was taken as a sign to hurry up my studies so that I completed elementary school almost three years ahead of time.

In *A Nemesis of Misgovernment* what impressed me most were the pictures of the Night Patrol of St. Petersburg, the bomb-torn body of Alexander II being taken back to his palace in a sleigh, a string of heads on the belt of a Siberian head-hunter, various marvels of the Czar's palaces, and a description (meant to horrify) of the rape of Jewesses during the Kishinev massacres. My sympathy was on the side of the injured, not only because they were of my own race (of which I was very early conscious, poetically at first and painfully later) but because I was inclined to sympathize with the underdog. Yet my indignation was swallowed up in the details, which the author with scrupulousness characteristic of a scholar supplied fully.

The incident occurred in my last year of elementary school in a history class. Because of my superior knowledge I shone especially brightly in this class, and since I felt more and more frustrated as I grew older by my discovering every day that I was not the center of the world, as my mother had done her best to impress upon me, I needed the compensation which my excellence in history supplied to me. The teacher didn't know this, of course. She was a young woman and to her I was simply the nuisance who always threw her class off balance. If she had been better balanced herself, she might have been able to handle me less drastically than she did. But she was not sure of herself, and I was the most serious challenge she had met to her experience. She had a large and unwieldy class of thirty-five or forty students, and that didn't help matters either. I didn't know how much she hated me until that day.

Every time she asked a question to which I knew the answer, I couldn't contain myself. I rose in my seat (we had folding chairs in school in which I could remain half-standing half-sitting) and waved my hand under her nose. One day she couldn't stand it any longer and told me what was on her mind. She asked a question of one of the students to which he didn't know the answer. I was on my feet immediately. She turned on me coldly and said, "Sit down. You're a pest!" That was all she said. I crumpled up, entirely deflated. My overthrow was complete. A few minutes later, she asked me a question to which I did not know the answer. I saw myself as the object of everybody's derision, and the battle for confidence which I was fighting was entirely lost.

Politics possesses two irresistible attractions for the immature mind. It enables that mind, bewildered by its first contact with a reality of infinite complications, to understand the world and to master it.

To enter politics (although the basic motive may lie in fear) requires not a little nerve too, for its object is to direct other men's lives for one's own purposes. But nerve was precisely what had been shattered in my own case by my teacher's crushing epithet. I went through high school stunned. I was still very much interested in history, but I did not sense the practical use to which my knowledge could be put. It was not yet a political tool for me. There were some socialists in high school, but I didn't take much notice of them beyond watching them gather in conspiratorial circles after school was over.

Once I did become interested in politics, I quickly went to extremes. Beginning with a mild shade of liberalism, I went in the space of a year through socialism into communism. My home was a good training ground for politics. Every evening my uncles and their friends gathered round the dining room table and discussed the events of the day. Their opinions differed, so that these discussions became very heated. Sometimes I was allowed to put my own word in. But when they saw the extremes to which my views were tending, I quickly became an outcast. They stopped talking to me.

A newspaper had played an important part in the development of my thought, a liberal paper of which I read the editorials and columnists devotedly every day. I found myself so much in agreement with them that sometimes my enthusiasm spilled over into letters to the editor. These were printed in their columns. Later, when I thought that I really had something to say and I wrote to this same paper, my letters were no longer printed.

Political clubs such as I belonged to, whether socialist, communist, or liberal, possessed an inestimable advantage for the growing mind. I regained all my lost confidence. I learned that I could handle myself adequately. My powers were recognized by others, and I recognized myself as an individual. I learned that I had abilities to persuade and to think logically. These were not extraordinary, but they were enough to enable me to hold my own in conflict. I was not feared but I was respected, and this respect pleased me much more than fear would have done. The truth was that I was conscious most of the time of holding myself back, of not driving as far ahead as my strength could have taken me. This was because I shrank from committing myself irrevocably to the cause I espoused. I took refuge in my small role in the organization, because it absolved me from responsibility. I wanted to observe and to criticize, and for both of these occupations I judged the obscurity of the sidelines to be best.

I learned more in the political organizations to which I belonged than I ever did in college. In fact, the chief value of my undergraduate years was that they brought me into contact with such organizations.

What was it that influenced me to join them? And after joining, what was it that determined the direction that my views took?

I remember that the novels of Upton Sinclair were the first important influence upon me toward radicalism. And I was not the only one to be influenced by him in that way. Later, when I met S. who was destined to be my political comrade for a time and my personal friend for an even longer time, the first topic of our first conversation was Upton Sinclair. When we had both confessed a taste for his work, we knew that everything else would be settled in its proper time.

Sinclair disposed our emotions favorably toward those who were trying to change society and very unfavorably toward those who were trying to keep it as it was. Since we youngsters were dissatisfied for one reason or another with things as they were, there was no great difficulty in persuading us that the men who were trying to change them were heroes. Imaginative books were the best possible propaganda for the socialist cause, because they disposed us emotionally toward the acceptance of intellectual theories which by themselves were academic and dry as dust.

Afterwards, in due course, there followed the more difficult books of Marx, the economic treatises and the political boxing matches. It was these latter that attracted me most personally. I loved to watch the spectacle of conflict. Still later, it was the romance of the revolution which enticed me, the history of the Paris Commune and the Russian Revolution, Lenin's ride through Germany in a sealed train, the Kornilov rebellion against the Soviets and its suppression, the thousand and one other historical details which the past had enveloped in a thick atmosphere of nostalgia. Motion pictures helped too. Particularly the blood-tingling films of the Russian director Eisenstein — *Potemkin* and *Ten Days that Shook the World.* So did music. I never heard *The Internationale, The Red Flag,* and other working class songs without "a quicker blood." I remember a May Day celebration when I came out of the subway station into Union Square just as a band was passing playing the strains of *The Internationale.* I felt completely torn out of myself with excitement.

But in addition to books and the other arts which combined to confirm me in the leftward course I had taken, personal contacts were also important. The chief of these influences was a red-haired college teacher, who was later imprisoned by the State of New York for perjury. A young man in those days, he found it expedient to grow a beard to set him apart from the student body. Perhaps the beard was also a tribute to his admiration for his Russian friends. He wasn't the only communist on the faculty at that time who had a beard.

He astonished us freshmen and gained our admiration by his powers of logic. His demonstrations convinced us that he must be cleverer than we were, and since he was a communist, communism must be the correct solution to our troubles. I was a socialist when I entered the class, and I suspect that my marks which were just a shade below superlative were due to that unfortunate choice. But as I succeeded in straightening myself out during the remainder of the term and came around gradually to the teacher's point of view, my marks showed a corresponding increase until, at the end, I stood at the head of the class.

He spoke with a slight stutter unless he spoke very slowly. I recall how he entered the room and began the lesson with a provocative question such as "How many in the class are in principle opposed to the killing of men?" If that formulation were not clear enough, he explained it further until at the end all of us humanitarians raised our hands to indicate our positive answer to his question. Then he began to ask innocent questions of us. We suspected no trap as yet. He asked whether we knew how many men had been killed in the construction of the Empire State Building. Or how many men had been killed at grade crossings in the United States the year before. Or whether we knew that insurance companies were able to predict almost exactly how many lives it would cost to build a structure of a certain size and how many people were going to be killed in the present year and the year following in accidents at grade crossings. We, of course, had not heard of any of these things. They took us by surprise and they shocked our sensibilities. We felt somehow as if our own hands were stained with blood, for weren't we constantly using bridges and buildings and all sorts of modern conveniences that had taken so many lives to build? There followed a question as to whether we were willing to give up these conveniences for the sake of our humanitarian principles. This time we weren't so quick to answer as we had been before. He had us in the grip of his pincers of logic. By the end of the period, few were left who were any longer against the taking of life on principle. The teacher had the same effect on us that Socrates must have had on his opponents. He mystified us and he thrilled us because he showed us the use to which the gray matter in our heads could be put. Before that, it had just lain there.

But there was always another motive in his mind when he did this. If he proved to us that, logically speaking, the end justified the means, he also made sure to tie this up with what was happening in Soviet Russia, which was violating every law of humanity for the sake of the great aim which absorbed her. Those simple exercises in logic cost more than one boy in the class his life. I knew a few myself who would never have been communists but for him. They went to Spain to fight for the Loyalists against Franco and, in the flush of their political enthusiasm, they were killed. He himself didn't go to Spain. His job was to send others. Later, he went to jail for a while when the authorities got wind of what was going on in his classes.

As for myself, the most important thing I got out of his class was the habit of looking up in the dictionary every word I didn't know. No other teacher had succeeded in making me do this. But he was such a stickler for exactness that it was the only way to get by in his class. I thanked him for it later on, not because I looked upon his fanatical pursuit of detail as any more admirable than I had felt it before, but because I found that there were a great many other people in the world like him, only some of whom were professional pedants. The only way of holding the attention and respect of such people was to be able to become immersed in the trivia of life.

Once I had become converted to communism, I began to act in what in everyone else's eyes was a very brave way. There was nothing self-conscious about this action. All that I had to do was to open my mouth and say what was bothering me. I was innocent of the world as yet and did not know exactly how dangerous this might be. It was not hard for me to become a student spokesman for communism, because, though there were many who secretly shared my views and not a few who could have expounded them better than I could, there was nobody who cared to become identified in the eyes of the administration as a revolutionary. I saw then that in order to represent a political viewpoint, it is not necessary to be the wisest or best person in the party; it is simply necessary to say fearlessly what is on people's minds but what they dare not say for themselves.

Professor O. was the Chairman of the Department of Philosophy at that time, and he had a beautiful Oxford accent as well as a melodious, deep voice. Knowing my views, which I frankly expressed, he chose me to address a lecture hall of several hundred students on the subject of Communism. I went to work promptly and prepared a speech of eighteen pages.

The seats of the hall were arranged in semicircular tiers and I stood on the lecture platform with the pages of my speech before me on a lectern. At first, I had to steady myself by holding on to it. I was frightened by the faces in front of me. If I had thought of the fact that behind some of the faces were minds that were better than my own, I would have been even more frightened. Professor O. himself took a place in the audience.

I attempted not only to explain the intellectual content of communism as clearly as I could, but I wanted to gain adherents for the party itself, and so I concluded my speech with a stirring exhortation in my best imitation of the *Daily Worker*'s political style, calling upon "the workers, farmers, soldiers, and students of America to rise and to throw off the yoke of imperialist capitalism and to establish a Soviet America."

I'd say that it took courage to do this, if I could also say that I realized the implications of what I was doing — the difficulties that such a speech was bound to get me in with the faculty throughout my college career and perhaps throughout my life in a society against which I was declaring war. Or if I could say that I really grasped the meaning of the words I was saying — what they were bound to mean in actual terms of life and death if they were taken seriously.

I can say none of these things. I neither knew nor understood anything vital about a world in which I thought that I understood everything. I was merely uttering words which had no real meaning to me and which I unconsciously assumed must be just as meaningless to everyone else. My attitude toward the most important concepts was not unlike that of a child toward building blocks which he can knock down at any time without really destroying anything. It would not be important to admit this now if it were not for the fact that there are more people than one cares to admit, and some of them in high positions, for whom it is also true that they are incapable of taking the words they say seriously or of apprehending their full meanings imaginatively. Surely I wasn't so stupid, and I did understand something, but what I understood in relation to the whole truth was like a surface in relation to a deep and solid object, or like the face of a coin, which is divorced from the thickness of its metal and the inscription on its reverse side.

All this was not known to my hearers, who either took me seriously and therefore could not imagine that I did not take myself seriously, or did not take me seriously and therefore did not bother thinking about the matter one way or another. To both of these types, the thoughtful and the thoughtless, I became a hero. The first attributed to me a bravery I did not have, the second a bravado I did not want. And each of them was wrong. I was neither hero nor bravo. I was merely a man in the dark struggling, and it was no enemy I was struggling with, as I imagined at the time. It was myself.

I became a public figure to my fellow students. I emerged from obscurity. But it was a false image of myself which achieved recognition. It was an image propelled by an energy directed towards an entirely different end and it happened to fit in for a moment with the preconceptions and prejudices of those who surrounded me. How many have mounted to the highest summit of fame through just such false recognitions? And, in a sense, is it not almost always destined to be so? Our real self is either buried so deep that it cannot be dug out or else it doesn't exist at all. It is something entirely apart from the material of which we are composed or entirely identical with it. The first is the view of religion, the other of science. There is no middle ground between these conceptions.

On the strength of my appearance in Professor O.'s class, I was invited to join a secret communist literary society, melodramatically named *Pen and Hammer,* of which the red-haired teacher who had initiated me into the mysteries of bolshevism was the president.

But my reputation was not based upon that exploit alone. Another took place on the day when a demonstration of students was being held in the center of the campus over a cause which escapes me now. My college years were all in the heart of the Great American Depression of the 1930's and there were constant demonstrations of students and clashes between students and the authorities. On this particular day, the whole class and the teacher were watching what went on outside the windows of our chemistry laboratory. It was in the afternoon, and we were supposed to be conducting an experiment. We heard the crowds of students shouting slogans and watched the speakers waving their hands, and the excitement in ourselves mounted proportionately. Finally I could not stand it any more, and I called out "Come on! What are we doing in here? Let's go!" The whole class turned to me, and the teacher turned too. I realized what I had done. I wanted to pull back my words from the air.

The teacher apparently was himself in secret sympathy with the revolutionary students, and though he hated me for exposing him to a difficult choice before the class where he was the visible representative of authority, he let me go with a mild warning. But word of what I had done got around the school and it increased my reputation for audacity.

I was extremely active politically during those undergraduate years. I went to meetings, distributed leaflets and pamphlets, and spoke on street corners from soap boxes, beer boxes, milk cans, platforms, or anything else I could get my feet on. I developed my voice, learned to silence hecklers, to render them impotent and ridiculous before the eyes of a crowd. I had a ready wit and I learned to handle myself in the midst of any rough-and-tumble that might develop. And always, quite aside from public activities, I talked to anyone and everyone

I met. Politics, I discovered, is talk. I learned to distinguish between different types of opponents and to judge the value of allies. I learned how to take advantage of weaknesses, and when it was advisable to withdraw my forces. I never grew tired of talking, of arguing and convincing. I found emotion to be my own strongest weapon. My logic was passable, and I could hold my own with it, but if things went badly for any reason, I could always call up the reserves of passion and a certain knack of stringing together words that had emotional punch in them.

I believed with a terrible earnestness in the truth of what I was saying, and while I held a person in my grip, he could not doubt it either. I put thoughts into the mouths of my opponents, and then I shattered their positions. I had never before felt so fully alive. Muscles of my mind came into play which had long been idle.

I even tried making a communist out of my grandfather. He hated the Bolsheviks from his experiences with them in Russia where he had learned that Bolshevism was the enemy of the Jewish religion as it was of all religion, and I think it broke his heart to see me become a communist. I tried to convince him that communism was the logical conclusion of the teachings of the Prophets, but he didn't listen to me. Like Mark Twain, I found the old man so obtuse I could hardly stand having him around the house, and it took me a long time to become as obtuse as he was.

My ignorance and pretensions in those days appear to me unbelievable. On July 30, 1934, when Hitler purged Roehm and other opponents within the National Socialist Party, I was on a farm with my mother. I wrote frantically back to my political friends in the city. I was terribly excited. I thought that the proletarian revolution which we had all been waiting for was beginning in Germany. I had not the faintest notion of what was going on. I was like the man in the game of pinning the tail on the donkey who gropes about blindly and finally succeeds in putting it right between the donkey's eyes! In my letters, I made very profound analogies between the situation in Germany (about which I was entirely ignorant) and events during the Russian Revolution of 1917 (about which I was almost entirely ignorant). My analysis was ridiculous, but it sounded good. With a little more training, I could have become a newspaper columnist, who generally makes an even smaller insight based upon fewer facts go a much longer way. For in politics it is impolite to remember what a man or a party said the day before. If that were not the case, most parties would have vanished long ago in the realm of sheer astonishment and disbelief. There are only two things which count in the matter—conviction on the part of the writer and a gift for camouflage.

I read the situation in Germany not for what it was but in terms of my hopes at the time. I knew nothing about Hitler or National Socialism except what the *Daily Worker* told me. Nor would the situation have been improved if I had actually read *Mein Kampf.* I wouldn't have understood it at all. For I would have started with an emotional bias against it, and nothing (at least not in politics) can be understood with the intellect alone. All I was aware of inside Germany in July 1934 was a commotion which I hoped was a revolution against the existing regime. Everything that was favorable to this interpretation I seized and dwelt upon. Everything else I rejected and did not see.

My communist friends in the city knew no more about it than I did. If anything, they knew less, and they were not as ingenious as I was in improvising rationalizations of our mutual desires. They looked upon me as a shrewd analyst and afterwards, when my ideas were exposed as the fantasies they really were, my friends hardly remembered and didn't hold them against me at all, for they still liked me and had faith in my ability and honesty.

The organizer of our local branch of the Young Communist League was an interesting person. He inspired confidence in everyone around him, and I should like to know just how he did it. It's quite easy to say that he had the gift of leadership. He did have it indeed. But what does that mean? What does it consist of? He did not have an extraordinary amount of personal magnetism. I do not believe that he could have convinced anyone of the correctness of communism who was not more than half convinced already. But he bolstered the confidence of those who already belonged to the fold and that was a function hardly less important. It was somehow quite evident the first time you looked at him or spoke to him that he was "a good guy." It inspired us to know that a character of that sort believed as we did.

Partly, of course, he owed his charm to our own enthusiastic eyes, which were only too willing to endow him with the best qualities. We assured each other often what a fine fellow B. was. But it never occurred to us to analyze just what we meant by that.

He was short, and though you could not call him stocky, he was solidly built. He stood upon the floor like a well-made piece of furniture. He stood squarely, and it wasn't easy to budge him. If he stood behind us, it added to our feelings of safety. He seemed to have strong nerves, and that is very important in a political leader when you are in agreement with his views. I have noticed that those individuals who exercise the greatest attractive power initially are not always men with strong nerves. They retain in their characters an element of instability, like unstable chemicals, which affect most strongly those around them because they themselves are wandering and incomplete. If they have any solidity, it is of an acquired sort, the sort that is gained only after an intense struggle for self-mastery. They strive to extract some sort of organization out of chaos. Their confidence is built over a hollow base, and the vacuum and incompleteness felt inside exercise the attractive power over the potential convert. Men who are complete in themselves rarely affect others sympathetically. They may excite envy but nothing else. When people are already in the movement, however, characters like B. play an essential role for them. The B.'s tide the rest over their inevitable, human periods of doubt. They confirm them in the correctness of the course on which they have embarked.

In college, I took part in every rebellion against authority, in every demonstration, every meeting, every outbreak. I learned to distinguish between the types of opposition that we had to face. There was the blunt and brutal type represented by the President of the college, who, when a military review which he was heading was disrupted by rioting students (among whom I was in the forefront), swung his cane against the head of the nearest student, who turned out to be standing next to me. The President then issued a statement to the newspapers in which he called us all "guttersnipes." That became a term of honor for us. We had buttons struck off bearing the legend "I am a guttersnipe" and we sold a few hundred of them on the campus where it became a kind of fad to wear them. The atmosphere of that time is called up with perfect clarity when I think of those buttons.

A conciliatory opponent was G., the dean of the college who was so frail that anyone could have broken him in half, and yet he was frightening because of the authority he represented. He was the kind of man who, instead of quarreling, put his hand on your shoulders and said: "Now, now, boys! Why don't we talk it over first?" He had a fabulous memory for names and faces — something on the order of those who can add up columns of six figures more quickly than a machine, or memorize whole pages of the telephone book. He made personal friends of most of the communist leaders; he used to help them out sometimes. He even lent them money. But in his defense of the social order, he was more reliable and important than the blustering president of the college. That unhappy individual, who died a few years later (I think that it must have been of sheer humiliation) was infallible at being able to excite the worst antipathies of the students whose guide he was supposed to be.

His greatest inspiration was to invite as guests to a student assembly, in a college where 85% of the students were Jewish, an Italian delegation of twenty-one fascist students who happened to be visiting America. It was on that day that I was arrested by college police for distributing leaflets urging the students to demonstrate against this gratuitous insult. The arrest probably saved my career at the college, for it kept me from participation in the riot which followed. This was so violent that a great number of the rioters were expelled from the college.

My passage from liberalism to socialism and finally to communism was hardly significant, organizationally speaking, because the societies to which I belonged were loosely knit and one was able to drop out of them without any noise. But to break with the communists was altogether different. Here, the organization was very tightly knit. It was like joining a gang from which you could only emerge feet first. There was no such thing as resigning from the party. If the going became rough and anyone objected to the way things were being run, he was expelled with all the formality and ritual disgrace with which a man was read out of the bosom of his people. In Russia, the excommunicated one was shot or sent off to some remote corner of Siberia. The reasons for my break with my comrades are a little difficult to assign. Fundamentally, as is the case always in politics, it was a matter of differing temperaments. There were communists whom I liked, but these didn't count for much in the organization. The leaders were all gray, humorless men whose primary qualification for their positions was the ability to take and to carry out orders from Moscow.

Some of my reasons for leaving were, of course, not at all creditable to myself, but they were nevertheless inevitable. With the kind of upbringing I had had, discipline of any sort was irksome, and communist discipline which resembled a strait-jacket was intolerable. Another factor was that a childhood friend of mine, whom I no longer saw frequently but who was fairly close to me in spite of that, belonged to the dissident organization of Leon Trotsky. At first, I hated Trotsky with all the bitterness with which the orthodox hate the heretic. I was ashamed of the fact that like myself he was a Jew and that he had, as I was taught by the party, proved a traitor to the cause of the working class. But there were other things working deep within my mind of which I was only dimly aware, and as the revolution did not come as quickly as I had thought it would, my dissatisfactions and impatience rose to the surface. The quarrels between the party and me began about small things. I disagreed at first on matters just to see what would happen. The rudeness with which they slapped down these tentative efforts enraged me, and I complained more loudly.

I began to read the opposition press, which no member of the faithful dares to do any more than good Catholics read the books on the Index.

They tried to silence me — first by persuasion and later by threats. But I am by nature very stubborn and opposition only serves to make me more so. I had opened my mouth to say what I thought inside the party as I had previously opened my mouth to say what I thought outside of it, and I wasn't going to close it until either my opponents were beaten down or I was. My weapons were all intellectual, but those who opposed me were not so scrupulous. A trade union organizer came down to our unit and threatened to beat me. I had made some progress with my view among friends who knew me, but this threat did more than anything else to gain sympathy for me. It was the human element in Upton Sinclair's novels that had attracted me to the revolutionary movement, and now I watched the human element in action within the movement itself. People who liked me as a person gradually brought themselves, under the pressure which outraged their individualities as my own had been outraged, to the point of believing that they agreed with my political point of view.

I found how difficult it is in politics not to lose track of the main issues and to fight out the principal battles along secondary lines. For example, my struggle began with such a basic question as the proper policy for trade unions and it ended with the comparatively minor issue of party democracy and the right of members to express their opinions freely. It is a fact well known in military science that battles are rarely fought just where one side or the other had intended that they should be fought. Most of the famous battlefields of the world, like Gettysburg, achieved their distinction in history through a purely fortuitous coincidence of accidental circumstances which forced one side to give battle and the other to accept it on grounds other than those on which they had originally counted.

The battle between myself and the party machine mounted in fury until it seemed as if I would take with me more than half the membership of my unit. But I discovered that nothing is certain in politics — least of all party members. At the last minute many of them drew back. They gave no reason for their defection. They didn't need any reason. I understood what it was that moved them back into the line from which my blows had shaken them loose. It was their fear of solitariness. They were spiritually comfortable in the communist life which they had chosen, and they were afraid of the outer darkness of conventionality into which we were going to be cast.

The climax was reached in my trial before my unit prior to my expulsion from the movement. It took place in the living room of my friend S.'s house (that same S. who had become my friend originally because of our common admiration for the work of Upton Sinclair). He was still my friend, but in political matters he found himself lined up on the opposite side from myself. In fact, he was my chief accuser. It was interesting to observe the relation between personal friendship and politics. The personal relationship was the more important thing, and yet in a crisis, friend could kill friend. He might regret it afterwards, but on the spur of the moment there was nothing more important than ideas.

In a time like ours, when the world seems to be weighted down by too many ideas, when the whole world threatens to go up one of these days in the smoke of an idea, it is hard not to wish sometimes that man could govern himself not by the gray and the abstract but by the palpable and the concrete.

In Céline's *Journey to the End of the Night*, the young soldier Ferdinand wishes that his mother were like a bitch with her instinct to protect her young. Then she would not have consented to send him off in order to defend something so largely unreal as The Fatherland. Who has ever seen, heard, smelled, or touched The Fatherland? But it is just such fictions that end by swallowing up mankind in order that they themselves might live.

So here was my friend S. prosecuting me. And here I was, defending myself against someone for whom, outside of his immediate role as my attacker, I had affection. It was all very dramatic, objective, and intellectual. No one threatened to beat me up. We came to do battle on the field of the intellect and our only weapons were the weapons of ideas. The District of the Communist Party to which we belonged sent down one of its most subtle representatives to combat me. For it was evident that without help, the local group of the faithful would not be able to put me down. He spoke with a slight foreign accent, because he had apparently come from Russia not too long ago, and he spoke calmly, with the kind of patronizing patience that grown-ups often show towards children. His attitude was that his hearers were in danger of being led astray by someone incurably vicious. He had no hope of regenerating me. But he did want to save the rest.

I came to the meeting with a number of heavy volumes of the collected works of Lenin under my arm. With my heavy glasses, bent spine, thinness, and general air of unkemptness, I was a picture of the Radical Intellectual coming to defend himself. I had been studying all night long what it was that I would say. I had read over and over again the relevant passages in the works of the international founder of our party in order to present them to the other members. I put myself in the position of Lenin. What would he have done in a situation similar to mine, I asked myself, and I came to the conclusion naturally that he would have done the same thing that I was doing.

I was the first Trotskyite on the campus, and my historical and documentary interest by themselves were sufficient to make me attract attention. It was just around the time of the first Moscow trials, and this too shed an attractive romantic aura around my dissidence. I was hated by my former comrades, ostracized, and pointed out to the passerby as a curiosity. Years later, I was told by someone who eventually became a friend of mine that the first time he saw me at college, he had felt frightened — such were the lurid tales that had been spread about me. I didn't suspect that I had inspired any such feelings. I just went about my ordinary business and, as the only representative of my point of view among the student body, I was invited to contribute articles to magazines defending it, to participate in forums, to speak to possible new converts. I handed out leaflets, mimeographed a student bulletin, and spoke on street corners again. There grew up around me a circle of people who responded to my type of rhetoric and understood intuitively the emotional logic with which I defended my beliefs.

It was during this period especially that the philosophy of Marxism exercised its greatest influence over me in all realms of life. When I responded to literature or art or music, it was in terms of Marxist categories and explanations that I saw them. It was not only my views of society and government that were affected. It was every realm of human interest and discourse. I wrote essays on Marxian criticism; I delivered lectures on the Marxist interpretation of literature. In this I was helped by the fact that Leon Trotsky, whom I now accepted as my leader, was not only a great politician but a great writer as well. His style was of incomparable brilliance and his sympathies in the field of literature were as wide as they were discerning. It was he who directed my attention first to the work of Céline. Trotsky's *Literature and Revolution* was a kind of bible to me in those days. It is a remarkable book in every sense of the word; it is remarkably well-written and it is remarkably perceptive — not to speak of the fact that much of the material which went into its making was prepared by Trotsky while he was directing the armies of the Revolution. He still found time in those days to read the latest and most advanced novels from Moscow and Paris.

But at the same time as I thought myself a thoroughgoing Marxist and tried with all my might to integrate my world-view with Trotsky's ideas, other parts of my experience clamored for expression, and I was not fanatical enough to deny their rightful claims. I had always had a weakness for the philosophy of Schopenhauer—not only because his pessimism suited my usual mood but because he knew how to express himself as a poet. I even tried to make a difficult reconciliation between the ideas of Marx and Schopenhauer. This I did by saying that Marx was merely for the present hour, to ameliorate existing conditions, but Schopenhauer was for all time, the discoverer of those black truths about life that could not be denied. And as my witness, I took Marx himself who had said somewhere in his works that under communism man would suffer not as an animal but as a human being. That convinced me that Marx, at least, did not dose himself, as some of his followers had done, with over-optimism. Marx did not deny that suffering is the ultimate truth in life, but what he wanted to do was to grant man the leisure for education with which he might dignify his sufferings and raise them above the level of material necessity. Thus I put the aim of the Marxists graphically from an aesthetic point of view, when I said that it was to allow Proust to become a popular author. Today he was a luxury for the few, but tomorrow he would be given to the masses of people. That was all, I thought, that would be necessary; it was as simple as that. The mention of Proust here is significant, for it was Proust who dominated the part of my mental life at that time which was not given over to the revolution. His careful, aesthetic reaction to life was pleasing to my sensibility.

I did not stay much longer in the Trotsky movement than I had in the communist one or in the Socialist one before that. Divorce gets to be a habit—no less in politics than in matrimony. I was in love with an ideal, and that ideal in its completeness could not be found outside of myself. I proved to myself how true is the observation of Hitler that to an imperious temperament like his own, it was out of the question to join an organization which was large and stiff and not subject to much change. He had either to begin one of his own or to join one that was small enough to be stamped with the imprint of his own personality.

By far the most interesting of my experiences were in the smallest splinter groups. There, I got a kind of microscopic view of what went on in larger groups where the individual member does not grasp the pattern to which he belongs, because it is too large for him to grasp. Only the leaders of such groups ever see the whole thing in perspective. I belonged to groups which were small enough, so that every member could properly have been called a leader of them. We gathered in small rooms and parceled out the world among ourselves.

Local politics were too small for our consideration. If anyone had suggested that we interest ourselves in a New York City or state election, he would have been despised. Even national American politics barely entered the range of our vision, which could hardly encompass anything smaller than global thoughts. The hugeness of our conceptions was directly proportional to the weakness of our powers. We were like a paralytic, who has to compensate for the enforced idleness of his physical limbs by a corresponding development of his mental interests. Anyone listening to our discussions might have been terrified by the scale of our visions, and by the callousness and brutality with which we proposed to transform them into realities — until it was realized that we were actually powerless. Between some of our meetings, at least, there might have been a parallel with such as might have taken place in a lunatic asylum. Endless discussion took place on whether the next war between Britain and the United States would begin in South America or in Asia. If it were objected that Britain and the United States were friends, and there seemed to be no actual prospect of war between them at all, the objection would have been met with our contempt. It would have been quite obvious to us that such a person was naïve and knew nothing beyond what he read in the papers. We, of course, knew much more. We "knew" that the purpose of the papers was to screen the truth from us, and we also knew that it was an axiom of our particular kind of Marxism that Britain and the United States were rival imperialistic states whose clash was already overdue by a matter of twenty years. We could have brought a sceptic to a confused standstill by quoting to him certain little known facts about cartel arrangements, oil monopolies, and kindred subjects. Precisely because the ordinary person did not know anything about such things, he was likely to be impressed by them — at least momentarily. That is the advantage gained by surprise and novelty and explains much about the use of esoteric political doctrines even by the largest and most successful parties.

Another favorite subject for discussion was exactly where the revolution was likely to start in the United States. It was the opinion of the most erudite of our leaders that the midwest was the likeliest place because of its future industrial dominance of the country. And one bespectacled member whose wife was a school teacher and who had risen to the heights of revolutionary leadership from a more humble position as an instructor of ping-pong left for Chicago in accordance with the implications of this idea — thereby breaking up his home and causing his wife to divorce him. I saw him a year later back in New

York a beaten man, but I did not have the heart to inquire about what had happened out in the midwest.

There was a certain grandeur about these theorists, and I am glad of my association with them. There was a headiness in the atmosphere of those small smoke-filled rooms in which we dreamed and laid our plans. Anyone who hasn't felt the excitement of carving up the world just hasn't lived.

There was a letdown when our dreams came to nothing. But the letdown was gradual, while the illusion was sudden and overwhelming. It is surprisingly easy when you sit in a small room with men who believe as you do to forget that there are other men in the world, too many of them, who do not. For this human mind of ours with its limitless reach was especially made to contain illusions. Not all are as ambitious and grandiose as ours were, but almost all are detached at one point or another from the reality that exists. It is just a question of choosing the point of departure and trying to stick as closely to facts as our romantic natures will permit.

I had entered the radical movement alone and I left it again alone. It was like entering and leaving the world. The net result was that I was less lonely for a while. I went into and out of so many parties and organizations that I was bound eventually to end alone. Boredom plays a much larger role in human life and history than is commonly realized. Oswald Spengler was one of the few who realized the role which it plays. He predicted that Marxism would die not of refutation but of boredom.

For a long time, I held to the outward symbols of my revolutionary beliefs. If I were asked, I still said that I was a Marxist. But if further pressed, I had also to admit that I was a non-conformist. If I had had enough confidence in my point of view, I would have started a group of my own. But there was little use in that. I sensed that my beliefs were not strong enough to carry through for more than another six months or a year. I was in the stage of a love affair when the lover himself realizes that he will be healed by time.

My old enthusiasm flared up briefly once more. My old friend S., who had gone into the movement together with me and had been responsible for expelling me from the Communist Party, eventually joined me in my heresy and became a leader of the Trotskyite group. And while in this position, he became involved in a strike and was arrested. A civil liberties issue was involved, and I joined a defense group that was organized around him. It was purely a sentimental gesture on my part. I became very active again, but what I defended was not the politics of my friend, because I no longer agreed with him, but his right to free speech. Thus, the pattern that my rebellion followed against Communist Party discipline was now repeated with regard to the revolutionary movement as a whole. In both cases, I ended with a defense of abstract democratic rights.

That this was an empty, useless, and futile gesture did not occur to me till much later. It was like defending a man's right to sexual intercourse without any consideration of such an institution as marriage or such a feeling as love.

Echoes from my earlier life were heard long after it had ceased to exist for me. When Trotsky was assassinated in Mexico City — though I no longer belonged to his organization — the fact struck me as if it were a personal blow. I felt approximately the way the more sensitive conventional people in this country felt when Roosevelt died. I understood then the meaning of the events in Rome the night before Caesar's death described by Shakespeare, and the happenings in Jerusalem on the night of Jesus' death as the New Testament relates them. I was troubled all night by spectres and the most horrible dreams. The graves opened and gave up their dead, and the ghosts squeaked and gibbered in the cold air of Maine where I happened to be at the time. My whole world was shaken, and, in addition to dreams of terror, I had some wild dreams of sexual orgies too. I seemed to have lost control completely. I woke up feeling entirely exhausted. So I experienced during my lifetime the empty space which a great man leaves behind him and the terror which is caused by his sudden removal from life. The feelings and visions which we experience in such a circumstance are the greatest possible tribute to the importance of politics among men. Politics is the art (some insist that it is a science, but since it works, as art does, more by an appeal to the heart than to the intellect of man, I prefer to call it an art) of instituting order in the affairs of mankind. Without it no other activity could be carried on with any security or steadfastness of purpose.

There was an echo of my political interests again when Russia attacked Finland. All Marxists, even the Trotskyites, united in defending the indefensible action of Russia. They were forced to do so by their theory, and that showed me how ridiculous the theory itself was. According to the theory, Russia was a worker's state and, therefore, in any clash with a non-worker's state like Finland, we were not supposed to ask questions but to turn out on the side of Russia. But I did ask questions of myself. I asked how I could ever be on the side of a bully, theory or no theory. I perceived what many people in my position had lost sight of — that feelings come first and theories afterwards, and if my theories did not fit in with my feelings there was something wrong with my theories and they would have to be revised. I lived through again the drama of ideas which Pierre Bezuhov and Prince Andrey and other advanced young Russian intellectuals are shown by Tolstoy to have lived through in the year 1812. Theoretically, they were on the side of Napoleon — they liked his progressive ideas and they admired his personality — but when he attacked their own country and people, they took up arms against him and helped to kill him. There had been something wrong with their abstract theories, too, which life had corrected.

It was my first vital experience of the importance of nationalism in the modern world. Previously, I had thought myself a complete internationalist. I was a world citizen and I recognized only the world as my fatherland. I had forgotten that I was a Jew, or at least I had done my best to forget it. Now I saw what a hold local attachments and limited loyalties had upon me. These were the kind of loyalties that my grandmother had for her family, which I had once despised but which I now increasingly respected. For what does it profit a man, I said to myelf, to believe that he loves the whole world when he is disloyal to his own kin. In the communist movement, I had come across more selfishness and more callousness to the most ordinary and decent human feelings than I had ever come across anywhere else. What sort of saviors were these, I thought, who lied and cheated and deceived. They were quick to see the most minute faults in their opponents; they were entirely blind to their own, but these were nevertheless gross as earth. I had ignored the faults as long as I believed that the communists were essentially noble characters who hoped to do nothing but good. I saw, however, that this was not so. Their high-flown idealisms were used to conceal the baseness of their natures. This was especially evident to me in their attitude toward sex where I saw comrade steal from comrade as soon as his back was turned. The absence of scruples which they decried in the bourgeois world was ten times as bad in their own case.

Finland brought all these thoughts to a head. The unprovoked aggression against a small and peaceful state by the large and heavy Russian bear, covered up as this treachery was by hypocrisy and rationalization, was merely symbolic to my mind of the entire revolutionary fraud of Marxism of which I had been the willing dupe for so long.

The great strength of the communists was that they had fulfilled a spiritual purpose within me and within many of their sincere adherents. Or, at least, we thought that they had fulfilled that purpose until their falseness had become plain. But the spiritual place

within, which they had filled so unsatisfactorily and temporarily, needed to be filled whether they did so or not. I became conscious of that
in the empty years that followed my break with Marxism both in theory
and practice (years that were empty, of course, of nothing save significant experiences). I became conscious that something else would have
to take its place—something that would be along the lines of more
limited loyalties which, being within ordinary human reach, would
end by being more effective and generous than the louder and more
pretentious loyalties had been.

—1948

Literary History
and Criticism

Walt Whitman:
Critical Reception
from 1855 to the Present

THE BATTLE FOR RECOGNITION: 1855-60

LIBRARIES OF CRITICISM have grown up around those literary works which humanity has found most challenging, but it seems safe to say that there has never been a book more intimately bound up with the history of its reception than *Leaves of Grass*. From the moment it made its appearance in the world early in July 1855, it was the destiny of this singular imaginative production which, the author later implied, was to be taken less as a work of art than as a piece out of a man's life, to be "enveloped in the dust of controversy."

In tracing the development of the conflict of opinion, there is a certain logic in grouping the responses around the dates of the nine successive American editions which appeared during Whitman's lifetime (1855, 1856, 1860, 1867, 1871, 1876, 1881, 1888, and 1892). The decisive years were those in which the first three editions appeared. In later years, as Whitman's fame grew without ever quite overcoming his notoriety, grave men of letters felt almost compelled to take sides either for or against his work, and they brought subtlety and erudition to the task. Yet the early reviews, though not as refined and analytical as some later criticism, retain a surprising amount of freshness and interest, if only because, as Anatole France suggests in *La vie littéraire* with regard to the classics, the early readers of a work alone are free and spontaneous in their responses to it. Later readers are to some degree constrained by the consensus that time has brought about, even when they are moved to rebel against it.

The first sign that the new book, as unconventional in its appearance as it was in content, would not fail to find its mark was given by Ralph Waldo Emerson in his famous letter to Whitman written from his home in Concord, Massachusetts, on 21 July 1855, about seventeen days, according to the most reliable calculations, after its publication by the author in Brooklyn, New York. The last paragraph

of the letter indicates that for a time at least Emerson suspected that
the book might be a hoax of some kind. There was no name of an
author on the title-page, only a picture of the supposed author in most
informal attire and pose (open collar, no tie, hand nonchalantly placed
on hip, workingman's shirt and trousers, tilted hat) facing it. The name
Walter Whitman was printed in tiny letters on the following page in
the copyright notice, and the name Walt Whitman appeared unob-
trusively in one of the odd verses of the book, like the careless signature
of a painter stuck away in the corner of his canvas and barely noticeable
at first glance.

Cicero observed caustically that even the most pessimistic
philosophers took pains to identify the personal authorship of their
dispiriting treatises, and Emerson's interest may have been aroused
by the contrast between the near anonymity of this volume and the
"omnivorous" egotism which seems to inform it. His letter, after more
than a century, still preserves the sense of excitement with which he
made his discovery. It may be comparable in a way to the experience
recorded by Keats in his sonnet on Homer, and it was historically
more important, not because Whitman is comparable to Homer but
because Homer should have existed on the map of the world's literature
whether or not Keats found him there in translation, while Emerson's recognition and encouragement were of incalculable importance
in placing Whitman there. It is certainly fatuous to assert, as the
Norwegian novelist Knut Hamsun once did in a lecture on Whitman
at the Copenhagen Student Union in 1889, that "if he had not received that letter from Emerson his book would have failed, as it deserved to fail," yet the letter no doubt served as a catalyst to hasten
a process that might otherwise have been slower.

The earliest printed notice of the book, written by Charles A.
Dana and published in the *New York Daily Tribune* on Monday, 23
July 1855 appeared before Emerson's letter could have reached Whitman, and its tone, while far from being as hostile and mocking as
some later reactions were to be, was less encouraging and more
equivocal than a sanguine author hopes for. The paper gave its notice
of the new publication a leading place that day and it was both liberal
in space and tasteful in its choice of excerpts from Whitman's Preface
and his poems, but its very opening sentence expressed an attitude
of critical scepticism concerning the worth of the author and, after
saying some better things later about his work, it concluded on a rather
pinched and grudging note.

The mixed feelings of Dana presaged, more accurately than the
enthusiasm of Emerson, the conflict which for so long has swirled about

the book. The ambivalence of Dana is echoed in a review by the New Englander Charles Eliot Norton, which appeared in *Putnam's Monthly,* published towards the end of the summer in which the book appeared, September 1855. We could hardly guess, judging from Norton's flippant tone, that, behind the visible scene of public print, he was, very soon thereafter, participating in another drama with regard to Whitman's book. On 23 September 1855, in a letter to his good friend James Russell Lowell, Norton called *Leaves of Grass* to his attention confidently with the assurance that the book must have something good in it to have recently "excited Emerson's enthusiasm. He has written a letter to this 'one of the roughs' which I have seen, expressing the warmest admiration and encouragement." The time was only a few weeks before Whitman permitted Dana to publish Emerson's letter to him in the *New York Tribune* of 10 October (which Emerson complained to Samuel Longfellow was "a strange rude thing" to do) and long before he caused a striking sentence from it ("I greet you at the beginning of a great career") to be embossed in gold on the spine of the second edition of the book in 1856. But if Norton had hoped to interest Lowell sufficiently to tempt him to undertake a review of the book, his hopes were dashed by the reply from Lowell on 12 October: "No, no, this kind of thing you describe won't do. When a man aims at originality he acknowledges himself consciously unoriginal, a want of self-respect which does not often go along with the capacity for great things."

Another New Englander, however, was less reserved. Edward Everett Hale undertook to review the book in the *North American Review* for January 1856. Apart from Emerson's letter, this was the most understanding appraisal that the book had received, and Whitman himself was so well pleased with it that he gave it the leading place in a pamphlet of advertisements for himself entitled *Leaves of Grass Imprints,* which was distributed with the third (Boston) edition of the book in 1860. But it is significant that, even then, the reviewer's tone, while admiring, is also defensive and somewhat apologetic. He concludes with the observation that "there is not a word in it meant to attract readers by its grossness, as there is in half the literature of the last century, which holds its place unchallenged on the tables in our drawing-rooms."

The polemical note sounds like an answer to the bombardment of abuse against the book's indecency which must have begun in conversation before it reached the stage of print. Since many Americans at that time, though independent enough politically, were still colonial in their cultural attitudes, the effect of the negative verdicts pronounced in the London periodicals is not difficult to imagine. The *Saturday Review* of 15 March, 1856 had concluded; "If the *Leaves of Grass* should come into anybody's possession, our advice is to throw them instantly behind the fire." More vehement and uncompromising still were the pronouncements of the (London) *Critic* of 1 April 1856:

> Walt Whitman is as unacquainted with art, as a hog is with mathematics . . . Walt Whitman libels the highest type of humanity, and calls his free speech the true utterance of *a man*; we, who may have been misdirected by civilisation, call it the expression of a beast . . . If this work is really a work of genius — if the principles of those poems, their free language, their amazing and audacious egotism, their animal vigour, be real poetry and the divinest evidence of the true poet — then our studies have been in vain, and vainer still the homage which we have paid the monarchs of Saxon intellect, Shakspere, and Milton, and Byron . . .

The reviewer concluded with the statement that the most generous assumption he could possibly make was that the writer was mad!

The review in the *Boston Intelligencer* of 3 May 1856, which Whitman thought representative enough to bind into an Appendix entitled "Opinions" printed in the second edition of the *Leaves* later that year, made a valiant attempt to surpass the billingsgate of these reactions overseas:

> We were attracted by the very singular title of this work, to seek the work itself, and what we thought ridiculous in the title is eclipsed in the pages of this heterogeneous mass of bombast, egotism, vulgarity and nonsense. The beastliness of the author is set forth in his own description of himself, and we can conceive no better reward than the lash for such a violation of decency as we have before us. The *Criterion* says: "It is impossible to imagine how any man's fancy could have conceived it, unless he were possessed of the soul of a sentimental donkey that had died of disappointed love."
>
> This book should find no place where humanity urges any claim to respect, and the author should be kicked from all decent society as below the level of a brute. There is neither wit nor method in his disjointed babbling, and it seems to us he must be some escaped lunatic, raving in pitiable delirium.

To compensate somewhat for these vilifications, those men who were most directly under the influence of Emerson — Moncure Conway, Thoreau and Bronson Alcott — confirmed the validity of their chief's appraisal of the new American literary phenomenon. As early as 17

September 1855, Moncure Conway, writing to Emerson from Washington after visiting Whitman in his home, said: "I came off delighted with him. His eye can kindle strangely; and his words are ruddy with health. He is clearly his Book — and I went off impressed with the sense of a new city on my map, viz., Brooklyn, just as if it had suddenly risen through the boiling sea." Later, at the end of 1856, in a letter to Harrison Blake, Thoreau characterized *Leaves of Grass* in a sentence that has often been quoted: "Though rude and sometimes ineffectual, it is a great primitive poem, — an alarum or trumpet-note ringing through the American camp."

Emerson himself, however, had soon begun to waver, unfortunately. Whether this was due to annoyance at the use to which his private letter had been put for publicity by Whitman himself or to the unrelenting power of the reaction which Whitman had evoked in many reviewers or to genuine doubts as to the accuracy of his own judgment, it is now impossible to say. But as early as 6 May 1856, in a letter to Carlyle, Emerson is clearly beginning to be of two minds about his new protégé:

> One book last summer came out in New York, a nondescript monster which yet had terrible eyes and buffalo strength, and was indisputably American, — which I thought to send you; but the book throve so badly with the few to whom I showed it, and wanted good morals so much that I never did. Yet I believe now again I shall. It is called *Leaves of Grass*, — was written and printed by a journeyman printer in Brooklyn, New York, named Walter Whitman; and after you have looked into it, if you think, as you may, that it is only an auctioneer's inventory of a warehouse, you can light your pipe with it.

What a distance separates these sentiments from the ones with which he had hailed Whitman ten months before ("the most extraordinary piece of wit & Wisdom that America has yet contributed. . . . incomparable things said incomparably well, as they must be. . . . the courage of treatment which so delights us, & which large perception only can inspire. . . . It has the best merits, namely, of fortifying & encouraging. . . .") The truth appears to be that Emerson, like others who have made important discoveries, did not succeed in holding on to his faith in what he had found. Despite all of his vaunted individualism (in theory he was as uncompromising as Ibsen when he said at the end of *Enemy of the People*: "He is the strongest who stands most alone!"), Emerson was as inclined as other civilized men to yield and conform to social pressures in matters of literary evaluation.

In his later years, Emerson hurt Whitman's feelings by his failure to include a single selection from *Leaves* in his anthology *Parnassus* (1872). Yet it was Whitman's feeling that, in the deepest sense, Emerson had not changed his mind about his worth since 1855, and in his talks with Horace Traubel in Camden, he added to the written record something that Emerson had said to him as they were conversing on the Boston Common in 1860. Sensing that Whitman, despite his brave demeanour, was feeling somewhat disheartened by all the clamour and controversy which surrounded his book, Emerson said, in an effort to buoy up his spirits: "You have put the world in your debt, and such obligations are always acknowledged and met."

After Emerson's death, Whitman's disciples (Traubel, Bucke, Harned, Burroughs, Kennedy, O'Connor) were often critical of Emerson's vacillations. It appeared to them that he had blown hot and cold. Some of his quoted sayings hurt, e.g. that he had expected from Whitman the songs of a nation and had got only its inventories. Yet Whitman himself never questioned Emerson's integrity or the indispensable service his spontaneous letter had performed in getting a sceptical public to grant him a hearing. In later years, he told Traubel mildly that even his own brother George had said to him on one occasion: "Hasn't the world shown you that it doesn't want your work? Why don't you call the game off?" Walt said he had remained silent in answer to the questions. But, as Felix Adler once said consolingly to Whitman, "readers must not only be counted; they must be weighed." An Emerson, though he were alone in his appreciation (which, fortunately, he was far from being), would always carry weight in the world's estimation. And in conversation, Emerson may on occasion have been even more rapturous in his recommendation of Whitman's merits than he was on paper; he is reported, for example, to have said to a friend in the first phase of his enthusiasm over Walt: "Americans abroad can now come home, for unto us a man is born!" Among the many "firsts" to be claimed for Emerson in Whitman criticism, the allusion in the concluding part of this sentence is the first known suggestion of a comparison, which appealed to William Douglas O'Connor and many other Whitman enthusiasts in the late nineteenth and early twentieth century between the American poet and Christ.

In retrospect, it appears that the most redoubtable warrior in Whitman's cause at the outset may have been none other than Whitman himself! Though it is doubtful that he ever heard of them, he acted in the spirit of the words attributed to Rabbi Hillel: "If I am not for myself, who will be for me? But if I am for myself alone, what am I?" He may have hoped, like all authors, for a receptive audience when, in his thirty-seventh year, he finally published a book, but he was mentally prepared for the bitter polemic that ensued. And he was too intelligent not to have realized that, like Molière's character George Dandin, he himself "had asked for it!" Without being bellicose, he could, when occasion demanded it, be stubborn indeed (as when he rejected Emerson's friendly advice on the Boston Common to meet his respectable enemies half-way by expurgating his own book). There was a marked vein in him of the phlegm and recalcitrance that Motley had noted in the Dutch character. In his seventieth year, he was to use a military image in describing the first publication of his book more than thirty years before. He described it as "a sortie," the success or failure of which would not be evident for at least a hundred years more. Perhaps the figure that should be employed to describe his action is that of a gambit in chess. Literature was a superior and amusing game which Whitman enjoyed playing seriously against the world, and once his gambit was slashingly accepted and countered by his opponents and a fierce struggle began around his boldly exposed position, he proved willing to defend it as strenuously as was necessary.

Not only was he prepared for the extremely risky and unauthorized use of Emerson's letter (at a time when he could ill afford the loss of his one influential friend or the additional obloquy to which his tactics exposed him) but he went to the length of writing at least three separate reviews of his own book and published them anonymously in different places: the *United States Review*, the *American Phrenological Journal* and the *Brooklyn Daily Times*. Since he made no effort to disguise his characteristic style, the truth was suspected at once and used against him by shrewd contemporary readers and it was officially proclaimed by his literary executors in the volume *In Re Walt Whitman* (1893) after his death. He may have been inspired in this dubious practice, which raises some eyebrows among students still, from having heard of the tradition that the poets Spenser and Leigh Hunt (not to speak of the actor Garrick) had, at various times, all written laudatory accounts of their own performances.

He went still further by adopting (or, it may be, inventing) a technique that has become common in twentieth-century advertising when he made use of the hostile and negative opinions of his book as well as the positive ones (some of them composed by himself) in an effort to intrigue the reader's interest and to compel him to sit in judgment for himself. He was determined, since he evidently would never be an unqualified success, to be at least a controversial one, for he had intuitively grasped the idea, put into words by Oscar Wilde, that the only thing worse than being talked about was not being talked about. In fact, it might have been Whitman whom Irving Babbitt was writing about in *Rousseau and Romanticism*:

> As for the lesser figures in the (Romantic) movement their "genius" is often chiefly displayed in their devices for calling attention to themselves as the latest and most marvellous births of time; it is only one aspect in short of an art in which the past century, whatever its achievement in the other arts, has really surpassed all its predecessors — the art of advertising.

Whitman's penchant for giving prominence to and reprinting almost everything that was ever said about himself and his work, no matter how trivial, obscure or worthless the source, annoyed even some of his greatest admirers and friends. It was John Addington Symonds who observed of Whitman: "Instead of leaving his fame and influence to the operation of natural laws, he encouraged the *claque* and *réclame* which I have pointed out as prejudicial. . . . Were Buddha, Socrates, Christ, so interested in the dust stirred up around them by second-rate persons, in third-rate cities, and in more than fifth-rate literature?"

The answer may be that it was out of such unpromising materials that Whitman managed in his lifetime to forge a reputation sufficient to attract the attention of Symonds himself though he was separated from him by thousands of miles of ocean and all the tiers of society. But the real justification of Whitman's unorthodox methods should have been, for Symonds, not the simple pragmatic one that they worked but rather the beneficence of the results they accomplished for him and many others. For the healthy spirit and universal sympathies of the American poet moved Symonds, according to his own testimony, more than that of any other book except the Bible. He was one of those readers for whom the *Leaves* seemed nothing less than a religious revelation.

> For my own part [he wrote], I may confess that it shone upon me when my life was broken, when I was weak, sickly, poor, and of no account, and that I have ever lived thenceforward in the light and warmth of it . . . During my darkest hours it comforted me with the conviction that I too played my part in the illimitable symphony of cosmic life.

If, as Whitman suggests in *Democratic Vistas,* the true test of a book is whether or not it is capable of helping a human soul, *Leaves of Grass* had obviously passed the test, and no persiflage or sophistication could erase that simple fact. That is the basic reason why it was able to survive the first five critical years of its existence.

AFTER THE CIVIL WAR: 1865-92

Whitman's record as a volunteer helper in the hospitals in Washington from 1862 on, recorded in part in *Specimen Days,* seemed to many to support the cause of his *Leaves* as well by demonstrating clearly that he was not a writer for whom words are cheap and that the doctrines of sympathy which he expounded so eloquently were of a piece with the conduct of his life. This may not have been a literary argument rigorously logical and pure enough to impress the young Henry James fresh out of Harvard who did not hesitate in dividing the man from the poet and condemning the latter roundly, but it did make Whitman some influential young new friends like William Douglas O'Connor and John Burroughs. As a partisan polemicist O'Connor's rhetorical talents were formidable, and in his pamphlet *The Good Gray Poet* he portrayed Whitman as a martyr in the cause of literature because of his discharge from a department of the United States Government on the pretext that he was the author of an indecent book. The portrayal was so persuasive to some contemporaries that Whitman is sometimes described to this day in American newspapers under the sobriquet bestowed upon him by O'Connor.

Whitman was helped, too, by the popular appeal of two of his "Memories of President Lincoln." The very unrepresentative, loosely rhymed and metred Song "O Captain! My Captain!" was soon anthologized and, despite its author's earlier unsavoury reputation, accepted into elementary schoolbooks. "When Lilacs Last in the Dooryard Bloom'd," on the other hand, impressed the cognoscenti of literature not only in this country but in England. In his study of William Blake, Swinburne magniloquently proclaimed "his dirge over President Lincoln — the most sweet and sonorous nocturne ever chanted in the church of the world." It is interesting to trace the stages by which he passed from this hyperbole to his fulminations in later life against the dangers of "Whitmania."

Henry James, however, underwent a change of heart in an opposite direction. From the scathing sentiments of his review in 1865 he proceeded to the relative benignity of his notice of Whitman's letters to Pete Doyle in the volume *Calamus* thirty-three years later.

There is also the well-known report by Edith Wharton of the positive enthusiasm of James's oral renditions of Whitman's verses in her autobiography, for which she chose a title allusive to one of Whitman's Prefaces, *A Backward Glance.*

Whitman's progress during this period was both a cause and a result of his being "taken in hand" by reputable publishers and impresarios. In America, Whitman seemed to gain in respectability by being admitted to the list of Osgood, though the publisher soon regretted his temerity and drew back before the threat of litigation on grounds of obscenity by the state's attorney. But the greatest "coup" for Whitman's admission among the poets of the English language was undoubtedly created by the publication of Selections from the *Leaves* edited by William Rossetti in London in 1868. Whitman "wept and fasted" before consenting to the expurgation that he had obstinately resisted in his own country. But Rossetti, in whom the friend and critic were almost indistinguishable from the impresario. finally prevailed with results so happy that Whitman and his disciples during his last years were inclined to romanticize the experience and to conclude from it that he was but one more illustration of the proposition that prophets are not without honour save in their own country.

The fact is that the most careful student of the growth of his reputation in England, Professor Harold Blodgett, has shown that the barriers to his recognition there were not substantially different from those which confronted him in the United States. But distance lent a certain enchantment on both sides, and the self-confidence of Whitman derived sustenance from the friendship of Rossetti, the politeness of Tennyson, the enthusiasm of Swinburne (before his radical recantation) and Stevenson, the visits and pilgrimages of Anne Gilchrist, Robert Buchanan, Edmund Gosse, Edward Carpenter and others. Signs of affection and esteem from the centre of the English-speaking cultural world certainly produced a stimulating effect upon Whitman's American reputation, just as earlier signs of rejection and distaste there had created a correspondingly depressing effect in the most cultivated circles on this side of the Atlantic.

The final validity of Rossetti's successful enterprise, however, must remain questionable. Of Whitman it may be affirmed by some who are what Scott Fitzgerald called "quick deciders" that if you've read one of his poems (especially if that one happens to be "Song of Myself") you have read them all, but it may also be said perhaps with as much truth that unless you have read all of his poems you have not properly read any one of them. No man gains more than he from the mass of his accomplishment rather than by any detail or example of it, however well chosen. All of his words throw light upon the meaning of each, and all of his poems do likewise with regard to each of them separately. No poet, for better or worse, is less *concentrated* in any verse or set of his verses, and if poetry is, as Amy Lowell once said, concentration, then those people are right (including herself) who feel that he may be no poet at all. No poet is less safely, justly or even fairly selected, excerpted or anthologized. And yet this hurrying world requires excerpts, selections and anthologies because it does not have the time or leisure to devote to the elucidation of any writer the attention which he requires to be fully understood. It may have been some such qualms about compromising his integrity that troubled Whitman about Rossetti's proposal of a volume of selections, and, despite the eventual happy outcome of the venture, he may well have been troubled, for, contrary to the dark suspicions and conjecture of Gerard Manley Hopkins, Whitman was a man of honour and far from being "a scoundrel."

CANONIZATION, KINDNESS AND SOME BRICKBATS: 1892-1914

With Whitman's death in 1892, a predictable process of beatification on the one hand and of demolition on the other began. Some critics, particularly academic ones, attempted to steer a more or less neutral course between these two extremes, but this was not easy to do because the passions of the partisans ran even higher at times than when Whitman himself was alive. He remained a source of contention. Hagiography was the first order of the day. Literary remains of the master, tributes, memoirs, a uniform edition of his collected works, including variorum readings — all this was the work of years, of lifetimes actually for his literary executors: Richard Maurice Bucke, Thomas Harned and Horace Traubel. Traubel's voluminous notes alone on the conversations, correspondence and day-to-day life of Whitman's last years have produced six books of over five hundred pages each (the last published in 1982) and the end is apparently not in sight yet almost a hundred years after Whitman's death. Symonds' valuable testimony was published the year after Whitman's death (1893) which was also the year of Symonds' own untimely death. The valuable and rare collection of tributes and reminiscences *In Re Walt Whitman* was published by the executors in the same year. Among the more interesting contributions to this volume was one from T.W. Rolleston, an Irish admirer and correspondent of Whitman's who was instrumental in helping to translate the *Leaves* into German and thus contributing to the spread of Whitman's European fame.

The year 1896 saw two significant additions to the record by disciples of Whitman, John Burroughs and William Sloane Kennedy. The initial posthumous period also saw a large number of cooler though still basically kindly estimates of his significance such as the one by William James. Close to this category and yet more neutral in its assessment is that of James's Harvard colleague George Santayana, who as early as 1890 when Whitman was still alive had indicated in a philosophical dialogue that he was of two minds about his subject, since he found that Whitman was an author capable of inspiring delight at the very moment he was provoking critical scepticism, not merely in different people at the same time or in the same person at different times but simultaneously within a person. Finally, this period witnessed some ferocious onslaughts against the poet, degenerating at times into *ad hominem* and personal reflections upon him and his work rivalling the worst examples of what had been said about him in the 1850s. These expressions came from those who felt too strongly to heed the ordinary amenities and the cautious Latin admonition to say nothing if not good about the dead. Examples are Max Nordau, John Jay Chapman, and possibly T.W. Higginson.

This period is so rich in examples of all these varying attitudes that we have been compelled, for reasons of space, to omit many items which are intrinsically interesting. We have included nothing, for example, from the disciple Traubel's six volumes of memoirs and reflections. We have likewise sacrificed enthusiastic selections from Edward Carpenter and James Thomson, the author of *The City of Dreadful Night*. Among academic appraisals of various degrees of admiration or hostility, we have not included anything by Bliss Perry, Barrett Wendell, William Peterfield Trent or Paul Elmer More. An *ad hominem* assessment that we regret not having the space for (one of several examples of its kind in different languages) is a 1913 pamphlet by Dr. W. C. Rivers entitled *Walt Whitman's Anomaly*, published in London and, according to its cover, restricted to members of the medical profession. Rivers has little if anything to say about the literary quality of Whitman's work; he treats it solely for the light it is supposed to cast upon its author's latent or overt homosexuality. This question (in relation to the *Calamus* section of *Leaves of Grass*) had been raised directly during Whitman's lifetime by Symonds, and Whitman had indignantly denied what he regarded as a shocking imputation. Biographers like Professor Gay Wilson Allen have maintained an agnostic attitude on the point, but Rivers and those critics who have followed him insist on the decisiveness of the internal evidence of the poems themselves to establish the abnormality of Whitman's emotional life. From the point of view of pure literary criticism, of course, this approach, wherever it occurs, represents a bizarre digression. It is a historical curiosity, however, that there have always been those who would reduce Whitman from being primarily a writer to his interest as a "case." *Ad hominem* and reductive views of literature (including the Freudian and Marxist varieties) are effectively countered by Marcel Proust in *Contre Sainte-Beuve* with the challenging assertion that "a book is the product of a different *self* from the self we manifest in our habits, in our social life, in our vices. . . ."

An inference from such a view seems to be that the determination of aesthetic and intellectual worth must finally rest upon some impersonal or objective ground as independent of the judge as it is of the one he judges, and also that it may be asserted with confidence only when arrived at by a broad consensus of readers, as widely separated from each other as possible in space and time. For this reason it has seemed appropriate to conclude this collection with an excerpt from Basil de Selincourt's penetrating study of Whitman, first published in 1914. This study has been widely recognized as outstanding, and many of its detailed observations still seem as sensitive, sharp and perceptive as anything written about Whitman before or since. Selincourt's speculative metrical analysis of the opening lines of "When Lilacs Last in the Dooryard Bloom'd," for example, opened new vistas in the appreciation of Whitman's instinctive technical verbal virtuosity.

It is perhaps as fitting to close this survey of the first sixty years of Whitman criticism with the concrete, practical aesthetic approach of Selincourt as it was to begin it with the broad, sweeping moral generalizations about the effect of the book and its content made by Emerson. Emerson's letter, Whitman later confided to a friend, presented him with something like "the chart of an emperor." How well he utilized the prerogatives granted him by the man whom, in the Preface to the 1856 edition, he saluted as his "Master," is the subject of Selincourt's critical inquiry.

WHITMAN'S RECEPTION OVERSEAS

Professor Allen for his volume *Walt Whitman Abroad* in 1955 compiled a bibliography of Whitman criticism and translations listing a selection of two hundred and fourteen titles from Germany, France, Denmark, Sweden, Norway, Russia, Bulgaria, Czechoslovakia, Latvia, Poland, the Ukraine, Yugoslavia, Italy, Spain and South America, Israel, Japan and India. Extensive as this listing is, it is hardly exhaustive if only because it leaves out China, about which, especially since the mainland went Communist, information may not have been available to Professor Allen. In the year that his book appeared, however, press dispatches indicated that the centennial of *Leaves of Grass* was marked in China by the appearance of a postage stamp honouring him. One may surmise that Red China's interest in Whitman was of a kind similar to that which explained his vogue in Revolutionary Russia, about which I shall have something to say a little later.

His fortunes in France, which so often sets the style not only in women's dress but in the arts (and which, significantly, has accumulated more Nobel awards for literature than any other country in the twentieth century) are particularly interesting. Some of the most fashionable names in late nineteenth century and early twentieth century France have been among his translators and critics: Jules Laforgue, André Gide and Valéry Larbaud, the translator of James Joyce.

Laforgue's attention to Whitman had been called by one of the French Symbolist poets, Stuart Merrill, who had been born in America. Laforgue published his version in 1886 under the title *Translations of the astonishing American poet, Walt Whitman.* André Gide was impelled to undertake a new translation of Whitman because he was dissatisfied with the idealized versions of Léon Bazalgette, which had become popular in France. Apollinaire wrote a fantastic surrealistic account of Whitman's funeral, supposedly on the authority of someone who had been there. But the turning point came in 1918 when Laforgue's translations were republished together with some by Gide and some by Larbaud who also contributed an important and illuminating essay which fixed Whitman's place firmly on the map of modern avant-garde and experimental literature.

The first seeds of Whitman's German fame were sown in 1868 by Ferdinand Freiligarth, the revolutionary poet who was a friend of Karl Marx and was a political exile residing in London when the volume of Rossetti's *Selections* appeared. Freiligarth reviewed it with boundless enthusiasm for the *Allgemeine Zeitung.* More effective was a monograph in German in 1882 published in New York by a German-American Karl Knortz. Knortz also collaborated with T. W. Rolleston in translating a selection from Whitman's poems, published in Switzerland after the German police had forbidden its publication in Germany.

As had been the case in France, the most sensational advance in the value of Whitman's "stock" in Germany came with the end of the First World War. Hans Reisiger published a new translation of Whitman in 1919 which, according to one reviewer, succeeded in making the American into a German poet. Thomas Mann described Reisiger's translation as a "holy gift" to Germany. In the wake of the Second World War, another translation by Georg Goyert, the translator of Joyce, evoked the enthusiasm of critics.

The growth of Whitman's reputation in Russia was given its greatest impetus by the Revolution of 1917, but it had begun a long time before that. Before 1900, Czarist censorship forbade virtually any mention of him or the fame he was achieving in western Europe. Nevertheless, the novelist Turgenev, who was an Anglophile, a traveller, and followed literary developments in the English-speaking literary world with close attention, was impressed enough with Whitman's work to translate some of his poems and offer them to an editor. Turgenev also appears to have spoken to an American writer in 1874 (quite possibly his friend Henry James) and to have told him that while there was undoubtedly a great deal of chaff in Whitman's work there was some good grain there as well. Tolstoy, too, though seemingly even more ambivalent on the subject than Turgenev, suggested the rendition of Whitman into Russian.

Nothing much came of these efforts, however, until 1907 when Kornei Chukovsky took advantage of a relaxation in Czarist censorship after the abortive revolution of 1905 to publish his translations from *Leaves of Grass*, which, by the year 1944, had gone into ten editions. Writing in 1955, Stephen Stepanchev said: "It would be difficult to overestimate the importance of Walt Whitman in the history of Russian letters of the past fifty years. Whitman's emphasis on pioneering, on building a new, democratic future, on brotherhood and equality elicited a warm response both from youthful Marxists and from partisans of a gentler, more middle-class orientation." After the Bolshevik Revolution, Whitman's poems appeared with an introduction by the Soviet commissar of culture, Lunacharsky, and his work became the major influence upon the futurist poet Vladimir Mayakovsky. By 1955, according to Stepanchev, "It is not an exaggeration to say that Whitman is now a Russian as well as an American author." Whitman's successes in other Slavic countries may perhaps be attributed to Russian influence, but some of them appear to have been achieved independently of it. In Czechoslovakia, for example, Whitman's poems were translated years before Chukovsky's epoch-making version was published in Russia.

Whitman was known early in the Scandinavian countries largely through the efforts of the Danish journalist Rudolf Schmidt. The Norwegian novelist Knut Hamsun, who was very critical of America, reacted against Schmidt's publicity for Whitman by writing one of the most satirical and amusing pieces ever penned against Whitman, but another famous Norwegian author, Björnson, was an admirer of his work, and the novelist Johannes Jensen, not only translated Whitman's work into Danish but made the protagonist of his allegorical novel *Hjulet* (*The Wheel*) a character modelled upon Whitman, according to Professor Allen. In 1935, K. A. Svensson brought out a volume of Whitman's poems in Swedish translation.

French critics are credited with first bringing Whitman to the attention of Italian writers. His first influential enthusiast in Italy was Enrico Nencioni, who succeeded in arousing the interest of Carducci and D'Annunzio. Luigi Gambarale published a slim volume of translations from his work in 1887; this was enlarged in 1890 and finally a complete translation appeared in 1907. After the First World War, Giovanni Papini produced an effective proselytizing essay on Whitman's behalf, and after the Second World War the brilliant and ill-fated Cesare Pavese published an essay that is accepted as the most perceptive criticism of Whitman by an Italian. This renewed interest resulted in a complete new translation by Enzo Giachino.

The Cuban journalist José Martí, who had heard Whitman lecture on Lincoln in New York, is credited with introducing him to Latin America in 1887 with an essay that was published in *La Nación* in Argentina and received wide circulation in South America. After the turn of the century, a Whitman cult came into existence in Spain, and a Catalan critic published a study of him and his message in 1913. Miguel de Unamuno published a sensitive and illuminating essay on Whitman entitled "*El canto adánico*" ("Adam's Song"), and the Spanish poet Garcia Lorca wrote a poem about him.

Whitman's manifest indebtedness to the Hebrew Bible for both his verse-form and his vision made his appreciation in that language natural. Decades before the establishment of the State of Israel in 1948, the poet Uri Zvi Greenberg was writing about him. In 1950, S. Shalom, a poet and journalist of Tel Aviv, explained why he had undertaken to translate Whitman: "Whitman's pioneering is very close to us, and so are his Biblical rhythms. To translate him into Hebrew is like translating a writer back into his own language." The best known and most ambitious translation of Whitman into Hebrew has been made by Simon Halkin, a poet, novelist and critic, who is a retired professor at the Hebrew University in Jerusalem. Professor Sholom J. Kahn of the Hebrew University, an American who has settled in Israel, has written perceptively about Whitman.

Whitman's work has exerted an influence, too, upon Yiddish

poetry, and Louis Miller has translated and published selections from *Leaves of Grass* in that language.

Appreciation of Whitman in the Far East may be explained at least in part, as the United States Ambassador to Japan, John M. Allison, once did in opening an exhibit of Whitman materials accumulated by collectors in Tokyo after the Second World War, as a simple human response to the outgoing affection so warmly expressed by the poet who wrote *Salut au monde*:

> Health to you! good will to you all, from me and America sent!
> Each of us inevitable,
> Each of us limitless — each of us with his or her right upon the earth.

In a country like India, however, another factor may enter in that Whitman's mysticism has been thought by some readers to resemble that of the Upanishads, the Bhagavad-Gita and other sacred books. This had already been noticed by a reader like Thoreau who asked Whitman if he had ever read these Indian texts which were just becoming familiar to the West in translation during the nineteenth century. "No," Whitman is said to have replied to Thoreau's query, "Tell me about them."

SOME AMERICAN CRITICISM AFTER 1914

In an article published in 1928 entitled "The Critic and American Life," Irving Babbitt recorded his own "protest against the present preposterous overestimate of Walt Whitman." In the same year, writing an Introduction to the *Selected Poems of Ezra Pound*, T. S. Eliot assured readers, who may have entertained doubts upon the point, that "I did not read Whitman until much later in life, and had to conquer an aversion to his form, as well as much of his matter, in order to do so." He added: "I am equally certain — indeed it is obvious — that Pound owes nothing to Whitman. This is an elementary observation." In the light of some scholarly and critical investigations since then, the truth of this observation has turned out to be neither obvious nor elementary. And Eliot himself may have recognized this when he came to write of Pound again in the 1940s. Amy Lowell, too, had felt compelled to deny the influence of Whitman on the Imagist movement in which she was prominent: "Often and often I read in the daily, weekly and monthly press, that modern *vers libre* writers derive their form from Walt Whitman. As a matter of fact, most of them got it from French Symbolist poets . . ."

The prevailing liberal and literary view of the period, though,

increasingly approximated the one which Ludwig Lewisohn formu-
lated with characteristic rhetoric and eloquence in his *Expression in
America* (1932) where he had called Whitman "the most strange
and difficult figure in all our letters and perhaps the greatest, certainly the most far-reaching, far-echoing poetic voice."

In the wake of the Great War (1914–18) many factors had con-
verged to give Whitman pre-eminent stature, at home no less than
abroad. The rise of America to world power heightened the interest
in the work of a man who had self-consciously proclaimed himself
her representative poet and had been accepted at his own estimate
by a band of energetic and capable disciples. In the paradoxical postwar world of Prohibition and affluence, those intellectuals leading the
struggle for liberation from the repressiveness and inhibitions of Puritan
legalism found his frankness and openness, particularly with regard
to sexual matters, much to their taste and honoured him as a precur-
sor for the courage and obstinacy of the challenge which he had issued
against respectable convention, Victorianism, the genteel tradition
and censorship in his time. And many of his fellow-citizens, particularly
those of recent immigrant origin, overlooking the nativist and na-
tionalist strains in his work, responded to his internationalism and
to his capacious conception of America as "a nation of nations" (as
he had called it in the Preface of 1855) in which none of them need
feel alien any more or be compelled to sacrifice any of their distinc-
tive cultural characteristics and background. Amy Lowell made a dour
observation that "it is perhaps sadly significant that the three modern
poets who most loudly acknowledge his leadership are all of recent
foreign extraction."

While expatriate Americans (like Eliot and Pound) and some of
the "internal emigrés" in the States who sympathized with them regarded him with distaste and suspicion for those very reasons, other
American writers who felt more at home in the melting-pot and were
not altogether lacking in talent and prestige continued to testify to
the pertinence both of his vision and his style. The most obvious example of Whitman's influence (and it may be one of those whom Amy
Lowell had in mind) was no doubt Carl Sandburg, who claimed the
whole Whitmanian inheritance — aesthetic, social and political — as his
own. This claim can be granted only in part, however, because the
extraordinary vivacity of Whitman's imagination and his verbal in-
ventiveness and mimetic precision (e.g., "The carpenter dresses his
plank, the tongue of his foreplane whistles its wild ascending lisp")
are never more impressive or clear than when they are contrasted with
the laborious effects achieved by even a gifted member of his "school"

such as Sandburg. The sweep of Whitman's majestic vision of America ("The United States themselves are essentially the greatest poem," he had written in the Preface of 1855) also came into possession of the imagination of a novelist like Thomas Wolfe, as his friend Scott Fitzgerald clearly recognized. Wolfe's dithyrambics to America and the American Dream (when they are separated from their context and grouped together as they are in the volume edited by John Hall Wheelock, *The Face of a Nation*) are quite evidently Whitmanian in quality though they are even wordier than Whitman and though Wolfe's lyricism is more prosaic and drags its plumes along the ground instead of soaring up into the empyrean of song. Yet the reader of Wolfe has the feeling that Whitman himself might have been pleased that his own national ("Unionist") vision had at last found a sympathetic echo in the heart of a Southern writer from the Carolinas.

One of the most impressive of the poetic proselytes that Whitman made in the post First World War period was Hart Crane, who addresses him directly as an inspirer in one of the sections of his epic *The Bridge*. Unfortunately, since Crane's ambitious effort was regarded by many academicians at the time as a dismal failure, his intended tribute to Whitman turned into something of a reproach to his master, as is clear from the comment of Yvor Winters in his review in *Poetry* (Chicago) in 1930. According to this reviewer, *The Bridge* merely succeeds in proving "the impossibility of getting anywhere with the Whitmanian inspiration. No writer of comparable ability has struggled with it before, and with Mr. Crane's wreckage in view it seems highly unlikely that any writer of comparable genius will struggle with it again."

This forecast did not prove fortunate, and Whitman continued to exercise his fascination upon leading poets of the twentieth century long after 1930, as is evident from a response of William Carlos Williams to my invitation to contribute to a celebration of the centenary of the publication of *Leaves of Grass* in 1955. In the letter accompanying his essay (printed in *Leaves of Grass: One Hundred Years After*), Williams called the *Leaves* "a book as important as we are likely to see in the next thousand years, especially a book written by an American."

Succeeding generations of poets and prose writers of varying degrees of talent and prominence from D. H. Lawrence and Henry Miller to Allen Ginsberg, Lawrence Ferlinghetti and David Ignatow have all supplied vivid confirmations of the continuing viability and potency of the Whitmanian muse. The sixties, in America, with their turbulence and social upheaval, were as hospitable to Whitman, and for many of the same reasons, as the 1930s. And whatever the future may bring, it seems safe to predict that one facet or another of his many-sided and even contradictory appeal will continue to interest readers and writers. It is not too soon to affirm that he belongs not only to history but to living literature as well.

— 1971

Charles Reznikoff's First Novel
By the Waters of Manhattan

THE TITLE *By the Waters of Manhattan* identifies Reznikoff just as the title *Leaves of Grass* (which remained the same over the years while the contents of the book grew and changed) identifies Walt Whitman. Both Whitman and Reznikoff are singers and chroniclers of the American island, the name of which derives from the language (Mannahatta) of its aboriginal inhabitants. Reznikoff's title also includes an allusion to the waters of Babylon beside which the prophet sat down and wept. The American Jew, who had been born in Brooklyn in 1894 and whose parents had emigrated from Czarist Russia some years before that date, evidently felt, like the hero of one of the novels of George Gissing, that he had been "born in exile." But the reader should not, on this account, be expecting a tearful immigrant narrative, for if Reznikoff was a student of the Bible he was also a student of another student of the Bible, the philosopher Spinoza. From this stoic master, he had learned neither to laugh nor cry but to try to understand.

The title served Reznikoff on three different occasions. In 1929, *By the Waters of Manhattan: An Annual* was a privately printed collection of prose memoirs and verse. In 1930, *By the Waters of Manhattan* was a novel published by Charles Boni in New York. Finally, in 1962, *By the Waters of Manhattan* was a little volume of selected verse by Reznikoff published by New Directions and the *San Francisco Review*. The 1930 novel (which is reprinted here) had been introduced by the poetry anthologist Louis Untermeyer; the selected poems thirty-two years later were introduced by the English novelist, C. P. Snow.

Though Reznikoff's novel was not a success in the marketplace, it did score what may be described as a *succès d'estime*. Untermeyer's introduction was enthusiastic and so were the reviews in *The Saturday Review of Literature* by the then well-known novelist Leonard Ehrlich and in *The Menorah Journal* by a young instructor at Columbia University named Lionel Trilling. But its most impressive recognition perhaps came to him in a letter from William Carlos Williams, who had been associated with Reznikoff, Louis Zukofsky and Ezra Pound in the Objectivist Press of the 1930's. In a letter to Reznikoff dated March 30, 1948 and found among the papers of Reznikoff after his death in 1976 (the Reznikoff papers are now housed in the Archive for New Poetry at the Library of the University of California in San Diego), Williams wrote: "A confession and an acknowledgment! In all the years that I have owned a book of yours, nineteen years! a book you gave me in 1929, I never so much as opened it—except to look at it cursorily. And now, during an illness, I have read it and I am thrilled with it and in this Flossie, who has read it also, gladly joins me. You know, of course, that it is *By the Waters of Manhattan* of which I am speaking. Why have you not gone on writing? Why do you not start again now? This book has so much in it that marks you as a first-rate artist that it is shameful of you not to have persisted. It is not by any means too late . . . I'm ashamed never to have read your book! It took an illness at that even now to make me do it. Such has been my life and I find that I was the loser by it not you—as too often happens when we are neglectful of others, we are the sufferers, not they . . ."

Lionel Trilling's assessment of the book was not much different: "Mr. Reznikoff's work is remarkable and original in American literature, because he brings to a 'realistic' theme a prose style that, without any of the postures of the 'stylist,' is of the greatest delicacy and distinction. But more important and by virtue of this prose style, he has written the first story of the Jewish immigrant that is not false."

American literature in general around 1930 seemed to Trilling to be suffering from a divorce between painfulness of subject matter and beauty of style—almost as if distinction of style were incompatible with sincerity. Literature about Jewish immigrants in America (and what soon came to be called "proletarian literature") seemed particularly to suffer from such a divorce, which resulted in a perversion of literary truth and a confusion of moral values. It was on this ground that Trilling preferred Reznikoff's book to the much more sensational and commercially successful *Jews Without Money* by Michael Gold, also published in 1930. "Mr. Reznikoff is one of a very small group of writers who have, by the skill of their writing, avoided this perversion and confusion."*

---

*The letter of William Carlos Williams to Reznikoff and Lionel Trilling's review of *By the Waters of Manhattan* in The Menorah Journal may be found in the volume *Charles Reznikoff: Man and Poet,* edited by Milton Hindus and published in 1984 by the National Poetry Foundation at the University of Maine Press in Orono, Maine.

Reznikoff's training had been in journalism and law. After graduating from Boys High School in Brooklyn before his sixteenth birthday, he enrolled in the newly established School of Journalism at the University of Missouri. He stayed there for only one year, disappointed at finding that journalists were more interested in news than in writing and that "news" to them meant, more often than not, sensationalism and melodrams of a man-bites-dog variety rather than the kind of "news that stays news," which was Ezra Pound's definition of *literature*. Young Ezekiel, who is the protagonist of *By the Waters of Manhattan*, expresses contempt for the kind of ephemeral "literature" which is seriously discussed in newspaper book reviews and bought by the impressionable public that is influenced by them. He gives, as examples of books that seem to him to have a more permanent claim to attention, the title of an Icelandic Saga, Thoreau's *Walden*, and a medieval romance, *Aucassin and Nicolette*. And it is possible to see *By the Waters of Manhattan* as itself divided into three parts which correspond to each of these examples: the first a saga of the Rubinow family in "the old home" in Russia and the early days of struggle in America, the second an account of a young poet's efforts to make a living by opening a small book shop, the third a romance between the twenty-one year old Ezekiel and one of his customers, Jane Dauthendey (whose family name is that of a minor German poet, though only Ezekiel realizes it, since Jane is unacquainted with her ancestral German language). Ezekiel is a very romantic and literary young man, indeed, in whose mind his own situation is constantly being assimilated to those he has read about in the classics. It is entirely natural for him and Jane to be thus transformed into Virgil's Dido and Aeneas.

After leaving the University of Missouri in 1911, Reznikoff worked for a time as a salesman in his parents' millinery business, while considering taking a doctorate in history. Eventually, however, he settled on the study of law, graduated second in his class from the New York University School of Law, and was admitted to the bar in 1916 at the age of twenty-two. A failure in his opening case on behalf of a relative soured him on the prospects of practicing histrionics in the courtroom. Instead, he put his training in the law to scholarly use in working for *Corpus Juris,* an encyclopaedia of law for lawyers, and to poetic use in writing the volumes of what he called *Testimony.* The close reading of cases, according to his *Early History of a Writer,* had a chastening effect on his own writing by teaching him the art of

prying sentences open to look at the exact meaning:
weighing words to choose only those that had meat for my purpose
and throwing away the rest as empty shells . . .
I, too, would scrutinize every word and phrase
as if in a document or the opinion of a judge
and listen, as well, for tones and overtones,
leaving only the pithy, the necessary, the clear and the plain.

At various times, he worked as a salesman, an editor of a small magazine, a translator, and—for a few years in Hollywood—as a general factotum to a friend of his, Albert Lewin, who was a successful producer at Paramount Pictures. These varied experiences are described in a posthumously published novel of his called *The Manner MUSIC,* found among his papers after his death.

Rereading *By the Waters of Manhattan* suggests to me that while all of its parts—the family saga, the search of the young poet for a means of livelihood, and his unresolved and unsatisfactory romance—have a claim to our interest, it is the last segment, occupying about a fifth of this short book, that is most sensitive and delicate and likely to repay our utmost attention.

The "affair" between Jane and Ezekiel (more Platonic than carnal) is a work of art within a larger work of art, and like other works of art it has many facets, which do not reveal themselves all at once but only to the attentive after a number of readings. Jane Dauthendey is the blonde offspring of a German father and a Jewish mother, who has bequeathed to her daughter only her beautiful dark eyes. That Ezekiel, who is aware of his own Jewishness with exceptional keenness, should at first take her to be a Gentile, is perhaps essential to an understanding of the development of the troubled relationship between them. The unresolved ending of the story, which may have frustrated the expectations of readers in 1930, when the theory of "open forms" was unheard of, may possibly have a different effect on readers more than half a century later, because it is an artifice which seems to have a greater fidelity to nature and truth than a more conventional ending, either happy or unhappy.

No one has quite captured the quintessence of what it means to love, but Reznikoff's effort may deserve comparison with the best efforts of the past. Only a poet, it seems to me, could suggest as much as he has done here. It is difficult to describe his achievement as either "romantic" or "realistic." The inconclusiveness of the ending certainly seems realistic, but the texture of the story throughout, if the adjective still retains any meaning at all, is romantic. Without any aid from the fascination of psychological analysis or the compelling interest produced by explicit sexual passion, Reznikoff manages to convey the mystery of the magnetic field of attraction that draws together into lifelong relationships highly individualized beings, who can never hope to communicate fully to each other their personal histories, which make them so hopelessly different from everybody else. The ending of the book points backward to its beginning. If the reader cannot help wondering what might come next, it may be more profitable to consider again what has come before. In the proper sense, no real beginning or ending would be possible or honest in a "saga" such as this. Nor does the word *continuum,* though more satisfactory as a description, do justice to its quality. There is some quality in Reznikoff's story which, like life itself, is not to be defined at all though it is unmistakably there.

On the most humble level, there is no question of the book's usefulness as a document and treasure-trove of immigrant Jewish lore. When Ezekiel recalls his mother's gloss upon the story of Noah in the Bible (the bird brings back an olive leaf to the ark to show that a bitter leaf from God is better than a sweet one from man), he reminds the reader of innumerable other Jewish mothers and grandmothers, who thus painlessly and unforgettably transmitted to their descendants the legends of the Jews preserved in the Talmud. The "old home" in Czarist Russia becomes the stuff of legend to one boy in a Jewish ghetto of Brooklyn in the 1890's, who hears of roosters living together with people and large enough to eat off a kitchen table!

There are locutions of speech in the book ("I wanna napple") which remind the reader of books like Henry Roth's *Call It Sleep* (published four years after *By the Waters of Manhattan*). Such attentiveness to the actual sounds of speech reminds us, too, of the indebtedness of both Reznikoff and Roth to James Joyce's *Ulysses.* We are reminded of the continual pressure of the Yiddish language upon the speech of immigrants when the father in Reznikoff's book tries to bring order out of chaos in his household by shouting out what is a direct translation of Yiddish idiom: "Let it be still!"

What helps to make *By the Waters of Manhattan* seem more true than other books of the same kind is that there are no apologetics or signs of "public relations" in it, nor are there any signs in it of the self-defamation that characterizes some American Jewish writing from Michael Gold (and before) to Philip Roth (and beyond). Reznikoff is always scrupulously fair, objective and detached, though he is never indifferent. A crooked Russian peasant who is an arsonist is balanced by a Jew who is a hypocrite and a cheat. During a pogrom, there are some Gentiles who take the side of their Jewish neighbors, and the Czarist government on occasion shows itself the common enemy of both communities. One of its ukases ousts Jews and Gentiles alike from land that has been designated as a military settlement. The pressure toward assimilation (which is produced not only by fear but by hope and desire) can be felt by everyone everywhere, even by those strong, self-sufficient, and self-respecting enough to resist it. Only the least sensitive may claim to be unaware of this. The writer is never self-righteous or hectoring, nor does he find a monopoly of virtue anywhere in the world or among any group.

There are continual reminders in this excellent prose of Reznikoff the versifier. Here, for example, is a paragraph, parts of which (with suitable modification of rhythm) he has elsewhere used in his poetry: "He heard the high-pitched conversations of the sparrows. He was glad that he was not Solomon; it is enough to overhear the speech of man, he thought. If he understood the chatter of birds too, the buzz of flies, how could he ever listen to himself? Then, as with a faucet, he turned off the thoughts splashing into the sink of his mind. He sat, a stone image, his feet on asphalt, overhead the long gray clouds, and looked quietly at the somber world. Men came and went. Still he sat there, his stone heart calm, his stone mind untroubled by thoughts, his stone fingers in his lap, his feet without walking to do. The noisy city rushed about him, a brook about a stone."

If in reading this passage one is reminded of Joyce's Stephen Dedalus in *A Portrait of the Artist as a Young Man,* one's second thought is about how completely Reznikoff has succeeded in integrating, absorbing and assimilating Joyce's influence upon him, unlike other weaker Jewish writers in whom the influence of the stronger makes lumps, like something too large that has been swallowed by a snake. Reznikoff as a poet can suggest the myths inherent in the prosaic world about him. There are passages in the book which may suggest to some of his American readers the theme of Hart Crane's *The Bridge,* published in the same year as *By the Waters of Manhattan*:

> He went down Broadway until he came to Chambers Street. He had not walked across Brooklyn Bridge since he was a boy. He made his way through the passage under the elevated trains, across the tracks of the street-cars, through the yellow darkness with its dim electric lights, the clanging of gongs, and the screech of wheels as the trolleys turned in loops.
>
> He was glad to find himself on the bridge, the tenements and office buildings behind him, his face toward the sky. Soon the

roadway changed to slats of wood, springy under his feet after so
many miles of asphalt. Ezekiel was pleased, too, after the even curves
of gutters and the straight lines of pavements and houses to see the
free glitter of the water. He was now in the rhythm of walking, that
sober dance which despite all the dances of man, he dances most.

Soon the bridge sloped to Brooklyn. Should he go on? He
remembered the dingy streets in which the bridge ended — and faced the towers New York has thrown up, climbing on steel and granite
from its narrow island into the illimitable sky. Ezekiel remembered
reading in the newspapers, when a child, that the Singer building
was to be built, and he had heard the riveters on many others. He
saw in these towers, already grown so familiar, the beginning of
a myth: men would confuse them, perhaps, with those of Camelot,
and through the millennia would look back at them with eager
eyes . . .

The poet in Reznikoff works together with the philosopher in him
to achieve a balance, which is an exceptional achievement indeed.
Sometimes this is done by carefully positing against each other
aphorisms and popular saws of opposing and even contradictory import, as in this passage:

> And her stepmother said, "In one place even a stone grows.
> You must stay in one place."
> Israel answered, "Change your place, change your luck. I have
> no luck here, I must change my place."

Such might be the dialogue anywhere between conservative and
radical. One speaks the wisdom of caution and tradition, the other
of adventure, innovation, and experiment. During the great economic
Depression after 1929, the equivalents of such a dialogue might have
been heard on many street corners of New York where the problems
of the social system and various schemes to improve or scrap it were
debated. It is no doubt to these discussions that Reznikoff is refer-
ring here: ". . . Some of those he had known at school were Socialists.
What good trying to change material conditions, if men are still the
same? But how can men better their spiritual conditions, if they need
their time and energy for bread? they would argue. To each his work,
he would think, they were too clever to let him escape in an ambigui-
ty, like a god in a cloud."

In 1930, there were not many young men like Ezekiel (who, we
must recall, was only twenty-two when the story ended, unlike his
creator who was thirty-six) who would have understood or sympathized

with such a philosophical attitude, based as it is on a conviction concerning the constancy of human nature and a definition of justice approaching Plato's, which counsels men to mind their own business rather than anybody else's. An American Humanist like Irving Babbitt, who did not enjoy much of an intellectual following in those days, might have understood him. But the times to many seemed ripe for Revolution, and this contributed its share to the failure of the book in the marketplace. *Jews Without Money*, which in its final page hailed the Revolution and the imminent collapse of capitalism, undoubtedly appeared to many who were not themselves Communists to be more relevant. Michael Gold appeared to be more forthright and topical. To the "red-hot fellows" of those days (to invoke Walt Whitman's colorful description of the Abolitionists of his own time) the prudent Reznikoff must have appeared somewhat stodgy.

But Reznikoff now has a second chance. Fashion was slow in finding him out. It was not till after 1962 that he began to be invited to campuses and poetry conferences in different parts of this country, in Canada, and even in Europe. Anthologies began to include his work. Literary historians awakened to the significance of the Objectivist school in American literature. The approval of elder statesmen among American poets, like Williams and Pound, stood him in good stead with their younger disciples, like Hugh Kenner. The poet Robert Creeley, in an Introduction to *The Manner MUSIC*, called him a genius, Hayden Carruth, reviewing his selected poems in *The Nation*, rubbed his eyes in disbelief: "I was captivated, enthralled, swept away — what is the word? Delighted, awed, roused. Really, I said, this is absurd, this is what happens to adolescents and young men in college, not to me; I had been writing, editing, reviewing books for almost twenty years. Nevertheless, there it is: I cannot exaggerate the degree of my enthusiasm for this book." Allen Ginsberg, who has preached the good news of Reznikoff's literary existence to his audiences for many years, entitled a set of his own verses, in tribute to his masters, "After Whitman and Reznikoff."

After his death, a publisher in California, John Martin of Black Sparrow Press, promised to bring back into print much of Reznikoff's writing, and has redeemed his promise with two handsome volumes of his *Complete Poems,* two volumes of *Testimony,* as well as *Holocaust* and *The Manner MUSIC.* The next volume which will appear is that of his little plays.

As we approach his centenary, his works have long ago proved their durability and fitness for literary survival. He has distanced ephemeral fashions and left them far behind. Now there is nothing left for him but to garner the lasting fame that so long eluded him, like many another worthy artist, while he lived.

— 1986

Whittaker Chambers' Witness

WHY SHOULD A NEW GENERATION of Americans be interested once more in Whittaker Chambers? Are the issues which engaged him, life and soul, still with us today? Does he have anything fresh to say that has not already been said and perhaps better said by others?

The answers to these questions are, at the same time, obvious and extremely elusive. Communism, as a forceful political philosophy that aims not merely to interpret our world but to change it beyond recognition, is unfortunately only too much with us. Therefore, the story of one man's journey to the uttermost depths of the Communist movement retains a compelling interest and relevance. It is not merely a part of our history; it speaks of something that has a potential for harm to those not immunized against it by terrible experiences.

Whittaker Chambers was both unique and representative. Even within the confines of the movement he espoused in his youth, he was drawn to extremes of faith and action where few of his comrades were prepared to follow. Yet there seems to have been an irresistible logic and no little courage in everything he did, so that his account produces a nervous shock of recognition among many of those who were preserved by some internal monitor or check from following more than part-way in the dangerous path he took.

The total and selfless commitment to Communism which he made for a long time led him to become the instrument of a foreign power bent on the injury and destruction of his own country's freedom. Yet how human and pathetic it seems that, in the turmoil of the actions and passions of his time, he should have been slow to grasp this. In the profoundest sense of the words, he did not really know the meaning of what he was doing or why he was doing it.

Under the devastating psychological impact produced upon him by the spectacle of the inhuman "show-trials" of old Bolsheviks in Moscow in the middle Thirties and especially after the unholy pact in 1939 between Stalin and Hitler (possibly in part because he was

89

himself married to a Jewish woman), he came to see his own perfidy in the same light as others were to see it later on. From this point, he brought to his shame, contrition and repentance for what he had done the same energy and courage that he had previously been misled into devoting to the Communist cause. Superficial sceptics and cynics may say of this change that extremes meet and that nothing resembles a hollow so much as a swelling. But this is to deny completely the difference between destruction and creation. Liberation and recovery from his Communist delusion resulted for Chambers in a remarkable flowering of useful and creative energies.

The climax of his contribution and restitution to America undoubtedly came in the years when he was simultaneously trying to work on the land of his farm in Maryland, hold down an important editorial job in New York, testify before a Congressional committee in Washington and grand juries elsewhere, and compose a confession and *apologia pro vita sua* of such high seriousness of political, moral, religious, and, yes, literary purpose that its equal has seldom if ever been matched in America.

Many underwent "conversion" to Communism in the generation of Chambers, and many became "deconverted" for roughly similar reasons. Many wrote books or essays about their experience of disillusionment and tried to analyze it. Few could write with the power, authority, and distinction of Chambers, and no one else perhaps was in quite the same strategic position to expose the clay feet of some idols to a tribe of self-styled liberal intellectuals which "controlled the narrows of news and opinion." The sensation resulting from his charge against such a pillar of society as Alger Hiss continues to reverberate into 1984 and has never been described more succinctly or brilliantly than by Rebecca West in an article on Chambers and his autobiography *Witness* in 1952:

> It was apparent that the [Hiss] case was being exploited for the benefit of the Soviet Union and to the detriment of the United States. By the side of the many upright men and women who sincerely believed in the innocence of Alger Hiss and said so for the highest motives, there was ranged another army uninterested in any sort of innocence. Whether Hiss was guilty or not, an extremely able general was fighting a campaign on the terrain of this case, with a double purpose. First, the public was to be persuaded that it was an inherently absurd notion that anybody could be a Soviet spy, that there was a Communist underground, that Soviet Russia had a secret service, that a person reporting a case of Soviet espionage

was thereby proving himself a lunatic or an impostor. Second, there
was to be created in the United States precisely the same distrust
of the law, the contempt for national institutions, the sense of pervading insecurity, which the Dreyfus case created in France . . .
It is doubtful whether it can yet be estimated how much damage
has been done to the courtroom.

The malevolence of the "liberal" response to Chambers thirty years
ago had to be seen to be believed, and (though in a somewhat dor-
mant state since) it has never quite subsided among those whose minds
had closed like a trap once and for all. The reaction can be traced
all the way from the mass of spiteful, partisan, malicious, insensitive
and imperceptive comment that surrounded the "witness" from first
to last and afterwards, all the way to the atrocious "docu-drama" seen
recently on public television, which purported to give us the scan-
dalous "lowdown" on what really happened between Chambers and
Hiss.

But it is time that we turned now from the ephemeral news of
the day, in which Chambers and his book have been too long mired,
to "the news that stays news," which we call literature. That is how
Chambers himself aspired to be judged eventually. In one of the essays
in *Cold Friday,* pieced together by a friend after the death of the author
in 1961, Chambers says: "Every book, like every life, is issued ultimately, not to those among whom it appears and lives, but to the judgment of time, which is the sternest umpire. What serious man could
wish for his life or his book a judgment less final?"

Thirty-two years after *Witness* was first published, it is increasingly evident how well it is likely to fare with posterity. If ever one
book were sufficient to justify the sufferings of a whole lifetime, *Witness*
is such a book. To read it or even to reread it (as I have recently found)
without being deeply moved is to argue oneself either hard of heart
or hard of hearing. Chambers outlived the publication of his book
by only nine years, but from the beginning there was evidence that
he had not missed the lofty aim he had set himself. He prized a letter
he received from André Malraux in which the author of *Man's Fate*
told him: "You are one of those who did not return from Hell with
empty hands." In 1961 Arthur Koestler said reverently: "The witness
is dead; his testimony stands." More than twenty years later, George
Will was comparing *Witness* to *The Education of Henry Adams.*

Rebecca West was virtually alone in grasping instantly that *Witness*
was not merely a book of topical importance but likely to become an
American literary classic. With nothing short of critical clairvoyance,
she perceived that "perhaps the greatest of all surprises disclosed by

the Hiss case [is] that Whittaker Chambers should be capable of writing an autobiography so just and so massive in its resuscitation of the past that it often recalls the name of the master of all autobiographers, Aksakov. The value of the book does not depend simply on its pain-fully exceptional material, nor on the sincerity of the author. Whit-taker Chambers writes as writers by vocation try to write, and he makes the further discoveries about reality, pushing another half-inch below the surface, which writers hope to make when they write."

The allusion to Aksakov may require elucidation, since the name is less well-known in this country than it is in England or in his native Russia. Sergei Aksakov, born in 1791, was a friend of Gogol, who inspired him to write autobiographical works, charming sketches of country life and sports, and reminiscences of his famous literary friends, which deservedly rank as classics among the great Russian books of the nineteenth century. It is difficult to imagine a higher compliment than to be compared with such a master, and Miss West, in truly magisterial fashion, details some of her reasons for doing so:

> [Chambers] admits the hideousness of life, writing of the madness of his grandmother and the despair and suicide of his brother as the calamities they were. "I used to wish that the house would burn down with all its horrors." But he also admits the beauty of life. That means that he can write tragedy. For he can give an account of a man who is visited by misfortune and include in it the reason he felt his misfortunes to be a breach of a firm promise made him by the universe. The particular manifestation of beauty which he took as a promise emerges during the book as a finely drawn character: as, indeed, the third protagonist in the Hiss case. It is a character which has appeared in other books, most notably, perhaps, in *Huckleberry Finn*. It is the American countryside . . . Some corrup-ting process, at work in all the older continents, seems here to have been suspended . . . He believes that nature is an aspect of God, and that to grow crops and tend herds is a means of establishing communication with God. He believes that he communicates with God and that God communicates with him. He is, in fact, a Chris-tian mystic of the pantheist school, a spiritual descendant of Eckhart and Boehme and Angelus Silesius.

Nor is this the limit of her insight. At the end of her essay, she pays Chambers what may be her finest compliment of all by comparing him to the French Christian poet, philosopher and Dreyfusard, Charles Péguy.

It impoverishes *Witness* to overlook in it the presence of Chambers

the young poet, accomplished enough to gain admittance to Louis
Zukofsky's Objectivist Anthology and enthusiastic enough to write
of his first experience of reading Walt Whitman: "It was not like reading
any other verse. It was as if by plugging up my ears, I were listening
to my own blood pound." *Witness*, in addition to its more readily ap-
parent political features, is a kind of Whitmanian love-letter to America
by a man who suffered greatly for his love yet is self-conscious (as
his painfully inward-looking verses on the tragic death of his brother
make clear) about wearing his heart on his sleeve. The Hiss defense,
leaving nothing undone, tried to play upon the jury's presumed distrust
of poets and read some of his verses in court, "trying [says Chambers]
to prove something about me that I never quite understood."

With the greatest examples of literary art constantly before his
mind's eye, Chambers was more conscious than any of his critics of
how far his own best efforts might be wanting. He apologizes gracefully
for any literary shortcomings that might be charged to him by way
of a parable based on his own lifelong admiration for a book by Victor Hugo, which he recognized to be far from perfect: "I think I can
hear a derisive question: 'How can anyone take seriously a man who
says flatly that his life has been influenced by *Les Miserables*?' I understand. I can only answer that, behind its colossal failings, its
melodrama, its windy philosophizing, its clots of useless knowledge,
its overblown rhetoric and repellent posturings, which offend me, like
everybody else, on almost every page, *Les Miserables* is a great act of
the human spirit. And it is a fact that books which fall short of greatness
sometimes have a power to move us greatly . . ."

Much of this is applicable to *Witness* itself. It is the truth of
Chambers, the truth particularly of his powerful feelings much more
than of his ideas, which carries all before it with the reader and makes
the book one of those rare literary artifacts that, in the words of Whitman, is "capable of helping a human soul." It is because the writer
has clearly paid with so much of himself for his book that it is the
one volume in the small library, which continues to grow about the
famous case, that is truly indispensable. I felt that to be so in 1952
and soon thereafter introduced the book on a reading list that was
compulsory in a general education course for seniors at Brandeis
University. A few years later, when Stanford University Press brought
out a collection of new essays on Whitman which I edited, I sent a
copy with an inscription to Chambers and received in return a
Christmas card with a note inviting me to call on him if ever I were
down his way in Maryland. I never availed myself of this invitation
but have not forgotten the kindness and courtesy which inspired it.

It is interesting to note that the pessimism pervading much of this book concerning the survival of freedom in this world and the ominous implications of its apocalyptic final chapter may have been somewhat modified by Chambers in his last years. In *Cold Friday* we find him reassessing world political prospects in the wake of Soviet satellite revolts at the death of Stalin, which occurred the year after *Witness* was published:

> Sudden solutions seems to me unlikely. Rather, force will work on force — who knows under what frightful multiples of pressure? The human forces will work on the inhuman dictatorship which they are in passive revolt against, so that the end result is more likely to resemble a new fusion of elements, rather than an abrupt reversal or displacement of one by the other . . . I am assuming, therefore, a process whose working out must, presumably, occupy the balance of the century. One taking place, moreover, in the absence of direct military action by East or West, in the absence of general catastrophe. I am assuming that there will be no world war, no apocalypse . . .

Whitman concluded his Preface to the initial edition of *Leaves of Grass* in 1855 with a far-reaching assertion of patriotic faith (the book seems actually to have appeared on July 4): "The proof of a poet is that his country absorbs him as affectionately as he has absorb'd it." In 1948, an American President scathingly described the Hiss case as "a red herring." Thirty-six years later, on March 26, 1984, an American President, who quoted *Witness*, conferred a Medal of Freedom posthumously upon Whittaker Chambers (the award was accepted by the Chambers' son John) at a widely reported ceremony at the White House in Washington. It is risky to generalize about the movement of history, yet it is possible to see in this event some indication that America, after long delays, is seeking to make some amends to the memory of one of her tragic and gifted sons. An even better amend may be to keep his words in print and to bring them to the attention of those who have never read him before or who have read him with insufficient attention. Writers who have given so much of themselves as Chambers deserve not only to be read but pondered and reread. In fact, as Nietzsche put it in Zarathustra, the writer who writes not merely with ink but with his heart's blood wishes not simply to be read but to be learned by heart.

Tomorrow someone may go further and bring back into life and print whatever of Whittaker Chambers now lies buried in the archives of periodicals to which he contributed some of his finest essays. As his appreciation of Franz Kafka's story *The Hunter Gracchus* in *Cold Friday* indicated, Whittaker Chambers was not only an excellent writer himself but a devoted lover of excellence in other writers, and his opinions of things literary and cultural as well as things political and religious, should long remain of interest to readers.

— 1984

The Achievement of
Irving Babbitt

TO DEFINE IRVING BABBITT'S central view of life, from
which radiate all his other views—of letters, of education, of
society—I begin by quoting not his own words, but those of a different
writer—one whom he would not have approved.

For in reading Bertrand Russell's recent autobiographical volume
Portraits from Memory, I encountered a passage—not without surprise—
that seemed to me extraordinarily close to the views of Babbitt as I
understood them, and which might serve as an epigraph to a study
of Babbitt's work. This passage occurs in a short sketch that Russell
wrote of his friend Joseph Conrad. In Babbitt's own terms, I had
previously thought of both Russell and Conrad as philosophical
"naturalists"—one a spiritual descendant of Bacon, the other as closely
connected with Rousseau. Russell was concerned primarily with
science, Conrad with sentiments. One was a utilitarian, the other a
romantic. Certainly there were important differences, too, between
them—Russell regarding himself as something of a radical, and Conrad
being regarded as something of a conservative. But both men had
been strongly contrasted in certain respects, to my mind, with Irving
Babbitt.

Yet reality is hard to pigeonhole. Babbitt himself makes allowance
for reality's infinite gradations and complexities when he attaches reservations to his most ambitious generalizations. He indicates, for example, that though he is highly critical of Rousseau's thought, which
he calls sophistical, it is with only one side of Rousseau's work that
he deals; and that undoubtedly passages may be produced from
Rousseau's writings that contradict what Babbitt takes to be Rousseau's
main tendency and influence.

This passage which I am about to quote, therefore, is not offered
as proof that either Russell or Conrad ever was a disciple of Irving

Babbitt; but rather that his point of view (which is consciously distill-
ed by him to its purest essence) entered as an element into their
psychological composition. Here is Russell's remark:

> He thought of civilized and morally tolerable human life as a
> dangerous walk on a thin crust of barely cooled lava which at any
> moment might break to let the unwary sink into fiery depths. He
> was very conscious of the various forms of passionate madness to
> which men are prone, and it was this that gave him such a profound
> belief in the importance of discipline. His point of view, one might
> perhaps say, was the antithesis of Rousseau's: "Man is born in chains,
> but he can become free." He becomes free, so I believe Conrad would
> have said, not by letting loose his impulses, not by being casual and
> uncontrolled, but by subduing wayward impulse to a dominant pur-
> pose . . . Conrad's point of view was far from modern. In the modern
> world there are two philosophies: the one, which stems from
> Rousseau, and sweeps aside discipline as unnecessary, the other,
> which finds its fullest expression in totalitarianism, which thinks of
> discipline as essentially imposed from without. Conrad adhered to
> the older tradition, that discipline should come from within. He
> despised indiscipline, and hated discipline that was merely external.

Though some of the images in which this passage is couched (for
example, the one of the molten lava lying just beneath the brittle crust
of convention) are highly charged emotionally and romantic, nevertheless the import of the passage is unexceptionable, I think, from
Babbitt's point of view and the remark about Rousseau is just such
a one as he himself might have made. Both the tone and the content
are analogous to those of Babbitt in *Rousseau and Romanticism*: "Though
strictly considered, life is but a web of illusion and a dream within
a dream, it is a dream that needs to be managed with the utmost discretion, if it is not to turn into a nightmare. In other words, however
much life may mock the metaphysicians, the problem of conduct
remains."

The problem of conduct — this is unfailingly the central concern of
Babbitt. On the matter of conduct, the world around Babbitt seemed
to him to have gotten completely off the track, if indeed the world
in general can ever have been truly said, with the exception of rare
men, to have accepted or even understood the true nature of such
a problem. With regard to ethics, the position of the ordinary man
may perhaps be compared to that of a passenger in a crowded subway train at the height of the rush-hour. He is kept upright not by
any conviction or virtue of his own but by the mere pressure of the

bodies around him. He is passive as far as the moral life is concerned, rather than active. But it was exercise and activity (possible inwardly even in that state of contemplative repose which paradoxically may characterize the "athlete of righteousness"); it was convictions and principles that interested Babbitt. Without consciously-held principles and convictions, the human being is little better than a brute. In an essay entitled "What I Believe," Babbitt once summed up the quality that seems to have disappeared from our contemporary world;

> Let us ask what it is that the modern man has tended to lose with the older dualism. According to Mr. Walter Lippmann, the belief the modern man has lost is "that there is an immortal essence, presiding like a king over his appetites." This immortal essence of which Mr. Lippmann speaks is, judged experimentally and by its fruits, a higher will. But why leave the affirmation of such a will to the pure traditionalist? Why not affirm it as a psychological fact, one of the immediate data of consciousness, a perception so primordial that, compared with it, the denial of man's moral freedom by the determinist is only a metaphysical dream.

Will is as much a key term in Babbitt as it is in Schopenhauer or Nietzsche. He devoted one of the appendices of his book *Democracy and Leadership* to this term alone. But it has a completely different meaning to him than it does to those philosophers. The difference is conveyed by the modifying adjective "higher." Babbitt's *will* is not primarily assertive — it is neither a blind will to live as it is in Schopenhauer (life as an end in itself, as an absolute, unquestioned value should be treated by Babbitt as agnostically as Socrates treats it at the end of *The Apology*: "To die and . . . to live. Which is better God only knows.") nor is it a will to power as it is in Nietzsche. It is a will directed inwardly against the subject himself. It is a will to refrain, a will to check oneself. Babbitt is lavish in praise for the restrictive classical qualities of decorum, proportion, restraint, and measure and for the synonyms and translations of these qualities which he terms "frein vital" (in opposition to Bergson's familiar "élan vital") and the "inner check."

An amusing story is told about a French auditor of one of Babbitt's lectures at the Sorbonne who is supposed to have exclaimed in frustration at the end of it the equivalent of "What the devil does this fellow mean with his 'inner check'?" Thereby this person showed (in my opinion, at least, though the story is repeated by those wishing to discredit Babbitt — as if he were to blame for the fuzziness of his key concept) that he himself was especially in need of understanding Babbitt's message. I do not mean that he was wrong in challenging the author of a piquant phrase to supply a definition of it. No one is more strict in his demand for definition and clarity in the use of terms than Babbitt, and one of his main objections to the romantics is that they discourage every attempt at definition. But there is something in the tone of the question that indicates that the asker of it would not have stayed for an answer.

The French skeptic was simply testifying to the fact that, since he did not feel anything in himself which corresponded to the expression "inner check," the words must be devoid of any real meaning. Yet the same kind of destructive criticism can be brought to bear effectively upon all philosophic terminology. Would that Frenchman, if he had been listening to one of Bergson's lectures, have cried out just as impatiently: *"Mais, que diable veut-il dire par cet 'élan vital'?"* I wonder! Perhaps he would. Yet the impertinent question is as unfair to Bergson as it is to Babbitt.

The answers to such unanswerable doubts are to be found not in any single sentence but in the writer's work as a whole. Babbitt's effort throughout his books is to supply a satisfactory meaning to the expression "the inner check" — parts of this effort may be detached from the rest provided that it is clearly understood that such a manner of approach to his meaning is only a makeshift. It is not by reasoning but by an immediate intuition that one approves or disapproves of the assurance of the pluralist philosopher (Babbitt's opponent) that life consists of "a perpetual gushing forth of novelties." In the same way, one feels or does not feel immediately (or else disguises from oneself that one feels) the weight of Babbitt's statement that in human life "there is always the unity at the heart of change."

What Babbitt means by "the inner check" could be illustrated from the writings of many authors, sacred and profane, whom he quotes. There is, for example, that favorite personage of Babbitt's, the Buddha. One of the striking verses of the *Dhammapada* reads as follows: "If a man conquer in battle a thousand times a thousand men, and if another conquers himself, he is the greater of conquerors." And then there is the passage from John Milton which reads as if it were almost a translation of Buddha's thought, though no doubt he achieved the same insight independently: "He who reigns within himself and rules passions, desires, and fears is more than a king."

It is the men who are able to learn and to transmit the profound and difficult lesson of self-conquest who become examples for the conduct of subsequent ages and not merely warnings (like those "bold, bad men" who have achieved historical notoriety). This is the true meaning of one of Babbitt's sterling sentences which seem to me to have few equals in the literature of his time: "In the last analysis, what a man owes to society is not his philanthropy, but a good example." That sentence appeared in an article entitled "The Breakdown of Internationalism," published by *The Nation* in 1915. A corollary of this point of view is to be found in his book *Democracy and Leadership*: "My own objection to the substitution of social reform for self-reform is that it involves the turning away from the more immediate to the less immediate."

A serious question with regard to Babbitt is whether, in preaching the archaic virtues of self-conquest and self-containment, he is motivated solely by the attractiveness of these ideals or by a perverse distaste for the expansive and aggressive (Babbitt calls them "imperialistic") ideals which have taken their places among his contemporaries. To put the question still more bluntly—is he being stubborn on the subject of Rousseau and romanticism because he is himself so deeply romantic perhaps? Is he not responding to the impulse to shock in a new and unheard-of way by embracing convention instead of being at odds with it? Is he not in fact part of the movement that has gone so much further since his time to "revolt against revolt"? Is it not possible, as someone has suggested, that even the quality of moderation may be emphasized immoderately? Doesn't Babbitt, in fact, himself belong with the type of enthusiast whom he treats so ironically in *Rousseau and Romanticism* "who recently went about the streets of New York (until taken in by the police) garbed as a contemporary of Pericles" but who was (according to Babbitt) "no less plainly a product of Rousseauistic revolt"? Wouldn't this Periclean enthusiast perhaps have labelled himself, had he been asked to do so, a "classicist"?

I do not believe that these are easy questions to answer, although I believe too that an answer is possible which should not be discreditable to Babbitt's reputation though it sees in him something which he was not sufficiently aware of in himself. He seems to me, in truth, to resemble his arch-intellectual-antipathy Rousseau in many ways. There are indications (in places he almost says as much himself) that Babbitt keeps hammering away at the themes of restraint, *frein vital*, inner check, proportion, decorum, and measure because he feels himself to be living—the more accurate expression of his feeling might be the word *drowning*—in a time when the anarchic freedom and license of the emotions are threatening to run away with us. Rousseau, on the other hand, thought himself to be living in a time when repressions and strait-laced corsetings of all kinds and especially of the natural feelings were building up to an explosion. Each was convinced that an important element of human nature was being neglected to the peril of humanity itself. Each responded to the needs of his time with a greater sensitivity to those needs than was to be found among his contemporaries generally, and each looked to the future to redress the wrong done to his reputation in his own age.

While Babbitt regarded the romantic view of life as fallaciously one-sided, he saw in its one-sidedness a reaction against the equally fallacious version of classicism which had preceded it. From this view follows his greater tolerance (at times, this amounts to genuine admiration — as in the case of Keats whom, despite certain reservations, he regards as so richly endowed as a poet) for the earlier proponents of the Romantic view as distinguished from the later ones. To illustrate this aspect of Babbitt's thought, we might compare his comments on Madame de Staël and on George Saintsbury. Madame de Staël's critical writings are regarded by Babbitt as prize examples of "Rousseauistic enthusiasm" and some of the comments he makes on them are accordingly hard — e.g., "She was unbalanced and did not escape the Nemesis that pursues every form of lack of balance." "Yet," he adds in extenuation, "it may be said in her behalf that the half-truths on which she insisted were the half-truths that the age needed to hear."

But no such justification exists in Babbitt's mind for the epigones of Romanticism. A hundred years make an immense difference apparently in the history of any institution or movement. In the essay "Are the English Critical?" Babbitt writes: "Professor Saintsbury is going on repeating eagerly half-truths that might have been a useful counter-irritant a century or so ago to the current conventionality and lack of perceptiveness, but which are an encouragement to the men of today to fall in the direction in which they already lean, that is, to plunge still more deeply into anarchy and impressionism." According to Babbitt, if the reader will forgive the pun, Staël was fresh but Saintsbury was simply stale!

The objection he makes to Saintsbury is one of the most serious he can make against an influential man — namely, that he flatters the conceit, indolence, and self-satisfaction of his contemporaries. This is such an easy thing to do. For example, he says in one of his essays: "Emerson transcended his time in important particulars, whereas President Eliot did little more than reflect the time in its main tendency. For forty years he pushed American education in the direction in which it was already leaning. His whole career illustrates the advantage of going with one's age quite apart from the question whither it is going."

The degeneration of romanticism since its obscure beginnings in the eighteenth century is summed up in witty fashion by Babbitt in *The New Laokoon*: "Judged by any standard Rousseau is a man of intellectual power, and he seems especially great in this respect when compared with Chateaubriand. Chateaubriand in turn appears an intellectual giant compared with Lamartine. Lamartine's ideas begin to look serious compared with those of Hugo. Hugo himself strikes one as intellectually active compared with Paul Verlaine. Traces of cerebration may be discovered even in Verlaine compared with some of the later symbolists. In these last anemic representatives of the school we arrive at something approaching a sheer intellectual vacuum — the mere buzzing of the romantic chimera in the void."

The decline in intellectual distinction and even in effort among the later representatives of romanticism probably accounts for their lack of realization that in repeating and embroidering upon worn-out formulas, they were merely taking the line of least resistance and not the one that was actually demanded by the deepest inner needs of their time. The idea that in any time there is a *main* tendency, which first has to be discerned in order to be evaluated, is an idea which Irving Babbitt has in common with his predecessor Matthew Arnold and with his successor, T. S. Eliot. An important sentence which Arnold liked well enough to repeat in two of his essays reads as follows: "Of the literature of France and Germany, as of the intellect of Europe in general, the main effort, for now many years, has been a critical effort." In one of Eliot's best-known and most frequently anthologized essays, *Tradition and the Individual Talent,* we find him saying: "The poet must be very conscious of the main current, which does not at all flow invariably through the most distinguished reputations." Similarly, in the very opening essay of his first collection, *Literature and the American College,* Babbitt has affirmed that "in an age as well as in an individual there are generally elements, often important elements, that run counter to the main tendency."

Arnold, Babbitt, and Eliot are equally certain of the existence of a "main tendency," of its importance, and of the necessity for analyzing it. This agreement itself I take to be something new in criticism, being the counterpart in literature of the historical and evolutionary way of regarding reality which increasingly dominated the thought of the nineteenth century and which is still so strong in our own time.

The feeling for "the main tendency" becomes a criterion for the judgment of men, forms, ideas. Emerson, for instance, according to

Babbitt (despite the side of his work which recalls Rousseau to mind) "remains an important witness to certain truths of the spirit in an age of scientific materialism. His judgment of his own time is likely to be definitive

> Things are in the saddle
> And ride mankind.

Man himself and the products of his spirit, language and literature, are treated not as having a law of their own, but as things, as entirely subject to the same methods that have won for science such triumphs over phenomenal nature."

Discovering, then, what he conceived to be the main tendency of his age and coming to the conclusion that it was a false and pernicious one, Babbitt set himself to oppose it as resolutely as Rousseau had set himself to oppose a very different tendency in the eighteenth century. Both Rousseau and Babbitt are men who *dare* — dare, that is, with full consciousness to move against all that is victorious intellectually in their own time. It was with reason, therefore, that in the first decade of the twentieth century when T. S. Eliot studied under him at Harvard, Babbitt was (according to Eliot's reminiscence in the memorial volume *Irving Babbitt: Man and Teacher* published in New York in 1941) "considered an interesting, eccentric, and rebellious figure amongst the teaching profession, and his outspoken contempt for methods of teaching in vogue had given him a reputation for unpopularity." In the half-century that has followed, partly due to that portion of Eliot's own influence which has been exerted in the same direction as Babbitt's, his ideas have come to seem less strange though they are still far from being dominant either in society at large or even in the academy, which might be thought the most fruitful soil for them to grow in, and perhaps they never will dominate.

But even those who have opposed Babbitt's tendency most vehemently (for example, Harold Laski in his book *The American Democracy* in which he concludes his discussion with the sentence: "With Maistre he could have said that the executioner is the cornerstone of society!") even Laski, I say, granted Babbitt the virtues of civic and intellectual responsibility: "With an obstinate courage he went into the market place to denounce with hot fury all the experiments, which his epoch attempted because they implied that there were no permanent standards . . ." Though the word *fury* is as ill-chosen as the comparison with Joseph de Maistre, the rest of the sentence is true — at the height of the public interest in the Humanist Movement in Babbitt's later years in the 1920's, he was called on to address as many as three thousand people at one time in Carnegie Hall in New York City.

Babbitt's professed purpose was steadfastly to oppose to the inadequate ideas of his age what he took to be the wisdom of the ages. He labored diligently to make himself worthy of Goethe's perfectionist advice and to bring to bear upon the aberrations of the historical hour the corrective supplied by the consideration of masses of universal history. He did this as objectively as he could and without rancor. Norman Foerster once recalled that in a quarter of a century of association with Babbitt he "never heard him speak maliciously of anyone." His interest in ideas was too pure ever to become bogged down with personal resentments. If his objectivity was tempered at all, it was not by coldness and disdain, but by warmth and generosity. Foerster recalls that "he was constantly coming to the rescue of his enemies, pointing out that their errors must not be exaggerated nor their virtues denied." In the measure in which he lived up to the high standards which he set himself, Babbitt doubtless will prove to be the beneficiary of the law he lays down in his book *Democracy and Leadership*: "A man who looks up to the great traditional models and imitates them, becomes worthy of imitation in his turn."

—1961

Babbitt's Masters of Modern French Criticism

JOUBERT, OF WHOM Irving Babbitt writes so sympathetically in this book, once remarked about Chateaubriand in a letter to Madame de Beaumont: "Notre ami n'est point un tuyau, comme tant d'autres, c'est une source . . ." This distinction of Joubert's is of the utmost importance. There can be no doubt that there are writers who are conduits of culture and others, much fewer in number, who are fountainheads from which the rivers of wisdom flow.

If Babbitt had been asked to which of these categories he belonged, he would probably have answered with characteristic modesty, that he belonged among the transmitters of culture. He seems, however, to me, one of the sources. By source I do not mean necessarily a "genius" in the romantic sense which Babbitt abhorred and taught his disciples to abhor. Such sources, once their novelty has worn off, are often seen to be nothing. Babbitt, on the other hand, though he appears at first glance to be merely expounding, interpreting, and criticizing the thoughts of others, turns out to have more important insights than the thinkers that he is considering. He is humble and makes no special claims to wisdom or originality, but neither did Socrates as he went about Athens questioning those who had the reputation for wisdom.

Babbitt is no peripatetic in the old sense. It is books that he questions, in this case the texts of the most celebrated French critics of the nineteenth century. As in his other works, he is primarily concerned in *Masters of Modern French Criticism* with the role of what he calls "the inner check" in our moral and spiritual life; he discerns the presence in human nature of a hitherto neglected impulse to "vital restraint" (or *frein vital*) which balances and sometimes overbalances that expansive impulse which Bergson identified as the "élan vital" — a concept, according to Babbitt, which exercised an unhealthy fascination upon the thinkers of his time. Babbitt deals here as elsewhere with the tripartite division of the planes of being into naturalistic, humanistic, and religious spheres. He is taken up with the problem of distinguishing between them and with keeping the middle area especially — that is to say, the humanistic one — from being squeezed out of existence by such logical pressures as Babbitt's student, T. S. Eliot, was to bring to bear upon his master's thought in the essay entitled "The Humanism of Irving Babbitt." Eliot's argument briefly is that between the naturalistic plane of being on the one hand and the supernatural on the other, there can be nothing but the vacuum of an excluded middle. The consequence, according to him, is that a humanism such as Babbitt's is bound either to be parasitic upon religion or else, as the case of another disciple of Babbitt's, Norman Foerster, seemed to indicate so far as Eliot was concerned, to fall back eventually into the naturalism from which it had striven to pull itself by its bootstraps.

Babbitt in this work is indirectly concerned with the problem of discipline in general, and with the distinction between sound conservatism and rabid reaction, with the relationship — either by attraction or repulsion, by sympathy or antipathy — between the thought of every one of the critics whom he treats and the influence of that "great father of radicalism" and modern sophistry in the eighteenth century, who was himself to be the central subject of Babbitt's next and most famous work, Jean Jacques Rousseau. Perhaps most important of all, Babbitt in this book tries to restore its original, etymological meaning to the word criticism — making its purpose to distinguish and pass judgment upon literary works rather than, according to the weak and inadequate, romantic conception of it in the nineteenth century, limiting its function to that of comprehending, sympathizing with, and communicating the purposes of the creative artist. At no time before this great critical century had the activity of criticism been so denigrated by other writers, and it may have been a measure of self-defense, therefore, that it refused to exercise its traditionally negative, judicial or veto power over artistic production. Babbitt came to change all that, and the literary history of the twentieth century thus far as well as its likely history in the future indicate that he was not altogether unsuccessful in attaining his aim.

Irving Babbitt was born on August 2, 1865 in the city of Dayton, Ohio. He was the son of Dr. Edwin Babbitt, who was interested in the problems of education and was the author of a number of obscure, quasi-philosophical volumes. The elder Babbitt has been referred to as a "crackpot" by the occupant of the Babbitt Chair in Comparative

Literature at Harvard, but the term seems to me much too strong to characterize a man who did not succeed in clarifying his thought sufficiently to gain much of an audience with the readers of his time. It is clear, however, from even a casual perusal of Edwin Babbitt's work that his ideas are basically at odds with those of his son and that he was principally inspired by New England transcendentalism.

The younger Babbitt graduated from Harvard in 1889, and at the age of twenty-four he must have been somewhat older than most of the members of his class. From the very beginning of his college career, he had exhibited evidences of that accumulation of vast stores of knowledge which was to be so impressive later on even to the most vehement opponents of his ideas. One of his college classmates, who was destined to become a well-known professor of French, recalls that Babbitt as a freshman, partly no doubt as a result of the positive tone which he always took, made so striking an impression of incipient pedantry upon the other students that within a week of the opening of classes he had been dubbed (by the Greek Chorus, which can usually be found in the last rows of any university lecture hall) Assistant Professor Babbitt.

After his graduation, Babbitt continued his studies at the École des Hautes Études in Paris where, under the direction of Sylvain Lévi, he laid the foundations of his knowledge of the Pali dialect of Sanskrit which enabled him eventually to make the translation of the Buddha's *Dhammapada,* which was published after his death in 1933. He had wished initially to teach the classics, but his relationship with members of that department at Harvard had apparently not favored this ambition, so that he turned his attention in time to the modern languages instead. He began his teaching career in 1893 as instructor of Romance languages at Williams College. After a year, he went back, in the same capacity, to Harvard, and there he stayed for the remaining thirty-nine years of his life—from 1894 to 1933. He did not attain his full professorship until he was forty-seven years old— in the year 1912, which is also the date of the appearance of *The Masters of Modern French Criticism.*

In addition to this volume and the translation of the *Dhammapada* already referred to, Babbitt published five other books: *Literature and the American College* in 1908, *The New Laokoon* (which Croce was evidently impressed with when he read it a dozen years after its first appearance) in 1910, *Rousseau and Romanticism* in 1919, *Democracy and Leadership* in 1924, and *On Being Creative and other essays* in 1932. After his death, his friends gathered together some of his scattered and unreprinted essays in the *Atlantic Monthly* and other magazines and published them in 1940 under the title *Spanish Character and other essays*. Finally, there was a memorial volume issued in 1941 by his friends, colleagues, and students entitled *Irving Babbitt: Man and Teacher*, edited by Frederick Manchester and Odell Shepard.

Some of Babbitt's best-known students at Harvard were T. S. Eliot, Van Wyck Brooks, Austin Warren, Norman Foerster, and Theodore Spencer. In the first decade of the twentieth century, according to the reminiscences of T. S. Eliot, Babbitt was an unpopular teacher at Harvard and his classes were very small indeed. Gradually, this situation changed. His weighty publications, which were the subjects of discussion in both the learned and popular journals, the increasing influence of students who had not forgotten him while making their own literary powers felt, and finally the almost accidental fact that at the time of the great economic crisis of 1929 and the years following, Babbitt's and More's ideas of Humanism, publicized by Norman Foerster and others, became subjects of controversy and debate almost on a level with ideas such as socialism and communism as well as nostrums like Technocracy — all of these things combined in later years to make his classes among the most popular and well-attended at Harvard. In his last years, it became the sporting thing to do for students in his classes to make betting pools, the winner of which came closest to guessing the number of authors (usually around fifty) whom Babbitt would have occasion to refer to in his lecture. His fame extended far beyond Cambridge, as an invitation to lecture at the Sorbonne attested.

The Masters of Modern French Criticism is, in a sense, a literary guide through an interesting part of the intellectual landscape of the nineteenth century. Like all guides of this kind, its aim is fulfilled only when it acts as a goad or incentive on the individual reader to journey up the trails which it indicates in passing. If, on the other hand, it is mistakenly regarded as an end in itself, its purpose is frustrated, rather as if a book-review, instead of whetting the reader's appetite, became a substitute for the book.

Babbitt's essays will have done their work properly when they have aroused our curiosity as to exactly what Madame de Staël, Joubert, Sainte-Beuve, Schérer, Nisard, Brunetière, Anatole France, and Jules Lemaître have had to say for themselves. After we have followed up some of the trails indicated, we can return to Babbitt's essays with added enjoyment and intelligent agreement or disagreement with the criticisms he makes. We should do even more and read, side by side with his essay on Joubert, the essays on the same subject by Matthew Arnold and Sainte-Beuve. He himself explicitly requests us to do so. We should compare his extended treatment of Sainte-Beuve with the essay in the third series of Shelburne Essays by Babbitt's friend and associate, Paul Elmer More, on the same critic. It is even instructive, as I shall point out later on, to compare some of Babbitt's criticisms of Sainte-Beuve with those in one of Proust's abortive rehearsals for his masterpiece, the posthumously published *Contre Sainte-Beuve*.

I have mentioned the names of Anatole France and Jules Lemaître in my list of those authors whose texts may supply collateral readings to careful and conscientious readers of this book, though the two are referred to only in passing and in the notes at the back of the book and are not themselves the subjects of full-scale treatments by Babbitt as are the other critics on my list. And this may serve to remind us that some of the more interesting and provocative things in this book are to be found among its notes. Whitman says somewhere that he has found a great deal of "poetic forage" in the notes to an edition of Sir Walter Scott's poems. Well, it would be no exaggeration to say that Babbitt has stored up a great deal of "critical forage" in the notes which he has appended to his book. Take, for example, his little remark on the name of Emile Deschanel, 1819–1904: "The paradox on the 'romanticism of the classics' that Deschanel maintained through several volumes does not seem of much significance for literary criticism." Does not this bare hint of an intriguing idea invite further exploration? Is not the "romanticism of the classics" a paradox which has occurred to other critics, if we will only consider it for a moment? In fact, is it not basically this paradox which, by accident or by intention, supplies the ammunition for Edmund Wilson's spirited onslaught against Babbitt in C. Hartley Grattan's 1930 volume, *A Critique of Humanism*? Wilson's little piece, entitled *Notes on Babbitt and More*, has been reprinted often since then, and it has undoubtedly helped to diminish Babbitt's reputation as a classicist to an extent. Is it not ironic that this should have been accomplished with the aid of a paradox that Babbitt buried in his notes because he did not think it "of much significance for literary criticism"?

Some of the author's dry humor is exhibited in the note which tells us that the prolific publications of the eager Emile Faguet, who produced as many as three and four books a year, "suggests a certain intellectual incontinence."

It is quite interesting, too, to come across a note of Babbitt's on Charles Maurras (a man with whom he has sometimes been compared by Eliot and others): "[Maurras] has actively defended classicism against modern laxity and corruption of taste, in such a way however, as to mix up the whole question of classic and romantic art with politics." In spite of Babbitt's modest disclaimer to completeness in his bibliography, there seems to be very little in the field that he has missed. I was interested to note, for example, that under the heading of Brunetière in his notes he has turned up a title by the little-known philosopher Alphonse Darlu, who has entered literary history before mainly because he was one of the most respected teachers of Proust at the Lycée Condorcet.

A comparison between Babbitt's essay on Joubert with those of Arnold and Sainte-Beuve on the same subject reveals that he is much more interested than they are in the ideas and pure thought of his subject, as distinguished from the man's personality. The account of the life of the thinker he is discussing is reduced by him to an absolute minimum. It consists of little more than the dates of birth and death (and, once in a while, the date of a radical change of direction in his subject's thought — e.g., the division of Sainte-Beuve's life into the years before 1848 and the years afterwards) and the dates of the publications of his principal books. Babbitt is uncompromisingly concerned with the intellect alone, and he is not interested (as even his fellow-Humanist Paul Elmer More was) in trying to make his subject "come alive" through colorful incidents or anecdotes which are irrelevant to his purposes. He is interested in him (or her) as *an expressive intellectual and moral complex,* which is a challenge to our analytical powers. This complex must be reduced to its constituent parts and related to the great tradition of humane and religious wisdom through the ages.

If he does not digress from ideas to even the most "fascinating" portions of his subject's life, it is still less likely that he will be diverted at any time to the life of the associates and friends of his subject. He is as far as possible removed from a critic like Sainte-Beuve whose interest in life is so great that it results in his giving ideas biographical settings of such ornateness as occasionally to engross all of our attention. Sainte-Beuve excels at sketching life-like pictures; even his individual portraits sometimes turn out to be group-paintings in which secondary characters prove to be nearly as interesting as his main one. He writes like a novelist manqué.

Take, as an instance, Sainte-Beuve's "Causerie" on Joubert. Several pages of it are occupied by his subject's charming, fragile, and unfortunate friend, Madame de Beaumont. Her grace, her illness, the very atmosphere in which this noblewoman lived and moved and had her being are all vividly evoked by the essayist. She was, he writes, "un de ces êtres touchants qui ne font que glisser dans la vie et qui y laissent une trace de lumière." Matthew Arnold does not go into great detail about Madame de Beaumont, but in a passage clearly inspired by Sainte-Beuve he describes her as "one of those women who leave a sort of perfume in literary history, and who have the gift of inspiring successive generations of readers with an indescribable regret not to have known them. . . ."

Such romantic exaggeration should, of course, be entirely out of character in Irving Babbitt. He is not an easy prey to imaginative enchantment of any kind. In his essay on Joubert, Madame de Beaumont is entirely absent except for one reference to a letter written to her by Joubert in which he discusses the quality of a Latin text of Immanuel Kant. He expects from his readers a familiarity with other treatments of his subjects from which such facts may be gotten. But Babbitt's concentration upon his subject's thought is a matter of both taste and principle. It is inconceivable to me that he should ever have written about Madame de Beaumont as either Sainte-Beuve or Arnold did. Her personality did not interest him very much. For him to have been interested in her, she would have had to be, like Madame de Staël, a woman of ideas. Babbitt is much more interested in the antipathy that existed between Joubert and Madame de Staël than he is in Joubert's friendship with another woman.

His objection to biography in criticism is a matter of principle, as we can see from a passage in an article on George Sand which he had published as early as 1898 in the *Atlantic Monthly*: "Taine says that there is in the whole history of literature no other writer whose career is as instructive as that of George Sand—no writer for the study of whose life there is such abundant material, and none to whom it is possible to apply so perfectly the method of Sainte-Beuve. The world at present shows signs of growing weary of the method of Sainte-Beuve as it has grown weary of naturalism; we are coming to be less concerned with the natural origins of a writer's talent, and more concerned with getting at this talent in itself, with measuring its absolute elevation, with finding out how far it is the product of the writer's will as well as of his environment. The life of George Sand lends itself even more to the latter method of treatment—the method of the new criticism—than to that of Sainte-Beuve."

So far as I know, this is the first reference to the "new criticism" which has recognizably been dominant in the literature of the twentieth century thus far—so much so as to evoke wild outcries and protests from men like Karl Shapiro. The "new criticism" was to be that of Babbitt himself, of his student, T. S. Eliot, and of all those who had learned the lessons of Eliot — Cleanth Brooks, John Crowe Ransom, and others — and who wrote for the literary periodicals in this country and in England in the twenties, thirties and forties of this century. For Babbitt, the life of a writer is no more than a framework for his thought — the frame may be drab and uninteresting, while the picture which it encloses may be interesting to the highest degree. We must never confuse art and life or allow one to distract our attention from the other. His objection to a critical method such as was exemplified by Sainte-Beuve and many of the critics of the nineteenth century who are studied in this book is that by confounding art, the intellect, society and psychology, it threatened the understanding which might be gained by a concentration upon any one of them separately. The same point of view basically is found in T. S. Eliot's famous essay in 1917 entitled *Tradition and the Individual Talent,* from which come the following familiar phrases: "The more perfect the artist, the more completely separate in him will be the man who suffers and the mind which creates. . . . Poetry is not a turning loose of emotion, but an escape from emotion; it is not the expression of personality, but an escape from personality. . . . To divert interest from the poet to the poetry is a laudable aim. . . ."

The insistence upon treating a work of art (or the intellect in general) as a self-contained (or, to use Eliot's word, "autotelic") object, which is an end-in-itself and has an existence entirely apart from its creator, was expressed not only in English-speaking countries but in France, too. A surprisingly close analogy to Babbitt's criticism of Sainte-Beuve in this book occurred in the long unpublished work by Marcel Proust entitled *Contre Sainte-Beuve.*

Here is the heart of Babbitt's contention on the subject:

> Criticism in Sainte-Beuve is plainly moving away from its own centre towards something else; it is ceasing to be literary and becoming historical and biographical and scientific. It illustrates strikingly in its own fashion the drift of the nineteenth century away from the pure type, the *genre tranché,* towards a general mingling and confusion of the *genres.* We are scarcely conscious of any change when Sainte-Beuve passes, as he does especially in the later volumes of the "Nouveaux Lundis," from writers to generals or statesmen.
>
> Yet history and biography and science are at best preparations for literary criticism, preparations that are always relevant to be sure, but likely to be less relevant in direct ratio to the distinction of the man who is being criticized. The greater the man, for example, the more baffling he is likely to be to students of heredity. The higher

forms of human excellence, says Dante, are rarely subject to heredi-
ty; and this God wills in order that we may know that they come
from him alone. The truth Dante thus puts theologically is, I believe,
a matter of observation so far as the past is concerned. As for the
future it is not yet clear that our schemes of eugenics are going to
outwit God. The genius of Keats is precisely that part of him that
cannot be explained by the fact that he was the son of the keeper
of a London livery stable. In this sense we may say with Emerson
that "great geniuses have the shortest biographies." "Can any
biography," he says, "shed light on the localities into which the 'Mid-
summer Night's Dream' admits me? Did Shakespeare confide to any
notary or parish recorder, sacristan, or surrogate, in Stratford, the
genesis of that delicate creation? The forest of Arden, the nimble
air of Scone Castle, the moonlight of Portia's villa, 'the antres vast
and desarts idle' of Othello's captivity, — where is the third cousin,
or grand-nephew, the chancellor's file of accounts, or private letter,
that has kept one word of those transcendent secrets? In fine, in this
drama, as in all great works of art . . . the Genius draws up the
ladder after him, when the creative age goes up to heaven, and gives
way to a new age, which sees the works and asks in vain for a
history."

The passage in Proust to which I should like to compare this is
in the eighth chapter of his posthumous *Contre Sainte-Beuve*:

Sainte-Beuve's great work does not go very deep. The celebrated
method which, according to Paul Bourget and so many others, made
him the peerless master of nineteenth-century criticism, this system
which consists of not separating the man and his work, of holding
the opinion that in forming a judgment of an author — short of his
book being "a treatise of pure geometry" — it is not immaterial to
begin by knowing the answers to questions which seem at the fur-
thest remove from his work (How did he conduct himself, etc.) nor
to surround oneself with every possible piece of information about
a writer, to collate his letters, to pick the brains of those who knew
him, talking to them if they were alive, reading whatever they may
have written about him if they are dead, this method ignores what
a very slight degree of self-acquaintance teaches us: that a book is
the product of a different *self* from the self we manifest in our habits,
in our social life, in our vices. If we would try to understand that
particular self, it is by searching our own bosoms, and trying to
reconstruct it there, that we may arrive at it. Nothing can exempt
us from this pilgrimage of the heart. There must be no scamping

in the pursuit of truth, and it is taking things too easily to suppose that one fine morning the truth will arrive by post in the form of an unpublished letter submitted to us by a friend's librarian, or that we shall gather it from the lips of someone who saw a great deal of the author. Speaking of the great admiration that the work of Stendhal aroused in several writers of the younger generation, Sainte-Beuve said: "If I may be allowed to say so, in framing a clear estimate of this somewhat complex mind and without going to extremes in any direction, I would still prefer to rely, apart from my own impressions and recollections, on what I was told by M. Merimée and M. Ampère, on what I should have been told by Jacquemont—by those, in short, who saw much of him and appreciated him as he really was."

Why so? In what way does the fact of having been a friend of Stendhal's make one better fitted to judge him? For those friends, the *self* which produced the novels was eclipsed by the other, which may have been very inferior to the outer selves of many other people. Besides, the best proof of this is that Sainte-Beuve himself, having known Stendhal, having collected all the information he could from M. Merimée and M. Ampère, having furnished himself, in short, with everything that according to him would enable a critic to judge a book to a nicety, pronounced judgment on Stendhal as follows: "I have been re-reading or trying to re-read, Stendhal's novels; frankly, they are detestable."

It is evident that in spite of similarities there is a world of difference between the impressionist Proust, disillusioned disciple of Anatole France and admirer of the philosopher Schopenhauer, and Irving Babbitt who held impressionism, skepticism and Schopenhauer in contempt and was an admirer of the solid classical merits of Boileau and of Samuel Johnson.

Proust explodes the critical pretensions of Sainte-Beuve by testing him according to a criterion which that critic himself had once proposed—the validity of his judgments of contemporaries. It is precisely in relation to his most significant and permanently interesting contemporaries, according to Proust, that Sainte-Beuve's perception failed him. He details a long list of his patronizing insensitivities to Baudelaire, Flaubert, Nerval and Balzac, as well as Stendhal.

For Babbitt, on the other hand, Sainte-Beuve's later coolness towards the stranger and more perverse blossomings of romanticism in the nineteenth century constitutes perhaps his best credential as a critic. It is likely that Babbitt's own attitude to Baudelaire, while not as extreme in its revulsion as that which he quotes in this book from Schérer, is not altogether unlike it. In other words, Babbitt finds fault with Sainte-Beuve because of the insufficiency of his classicism, objectivity, and detachment, while Proust finds fault with him for the insufficiency of his sympathy and insight so far as certain manifestations of originality in modern literature are concerned.

And yet when all these weighty reservations have been noted, the one striking point of coincidence between their views of the function of criticism still remains, and it is this point that served for the departure that, several decades later, became generally known as the "new criticism." Neither Babbitt nor Proust is as doctrinaire in his formalism as some later critics were to be, but they do insist upon a separation between the social personality, on the one hand, and the intellectual, moral and spiritual one on the other. From such a point of view, every work of the mind ought ideally to be approached as if its authorship were as unknown as that of the cave-drawings. The mastery of an intellectual discipline becomes comparable to excellence in the playing of a game — an activity which only very peripherally involves aspects of the player's personality other than his special skill. Eliot very early attacked what he called "the metaphysical theory of the substantial unity of the soul." Later on, he was to refer to poetry as "a superior amusement." Babbitt, of course, did not subscribe to this particular development by his disciple. For him, literature is anything but a game or a form of elegant trifling; it is its very depth and seriousness that set it apart from the ordinary business of life.

Finally, may I suggest to the student of criticism that he might do well to supplement the reading of this book not only in the manner I have already indicated but also by examining attentively a critical collection such as can be found in *A Modern Book of Criticism,* edited by Ludwig Lewisohn in 1919, which contains almost exclusively impressionistic texts, beginning with Anatole France and Jules Lemaître, and going on to those German, English and American critics who diverge as far as possible (though one of them, Spingarn, wrote a favorable review of *The Masters of Modern French Criticism*) from Babbitt's classical sympathies.

One would have to have a very sluggish mind indeed not to be provoked by a comparison and contrast of Babbitt's book and Lewisohn's into the most thoughtful reflections which might have a salutary effect in bringing to the surface and clarifying the reader's own assumptions about the critical function. I speak as one who has gone, over a number of years, all the way from the point of view so brilliantly expounded in *A Modern Book of Criticism* to the one which we find everywhere defended (implicitly, between the lines, as well as more directly) in *The Masters of Modern French Criticism.*

— 1963

Babbitt's Version of the Buddha's Dhammapada

IRVING BABBITT'S REVISION OF Max Müller's translation of *The Dhammapada* together with his almost booklength essay "Buddha and the Occident" was first published thirty years ago by the Oxford University Press, two years after the well-known Harvard professor's death in 1933. It was a labor of love to which he had devoted many years of his life. The founding father of American Humanism was interested in the most renowned of Eastern world-teachers while still an undergraduate at Harvard in the 1880's. As a fellow-student of his in those days, Professor William F. Giese recalled in the volume of memorial tributes *Irving Babbitt: Man and Teacher*: "He was already deeply immersed in Buddhism, and its influence in shaping his thought is so plain from the start that other influences (barring Aristotle) need hardly be invoked except as enriching tributaries. The ultimate convictions behind his humanism (which seemed then only an emerging aspect of his philosophy) are to be fully understood only in this Oriental light, however Aristotelian his analytic method. Buddhism preaches the extinction of all desire, and is thus radically anti-romantic. When, as a new-made bachelor of arts, he applied for a post as teacher, he jestingly consulted me as to the propriety of setting himself down as a Unitarian or a Buddhist."

Forty years later, in the 1920's, while studying with him at Harvard, Professor Victor Hamm set down his impression that "if Babbitt had a religion, it was certainly closer to Buddhism than to any other. Paul Elmer More, in conversation with me, corroborated this opinion, and the posthumous publication of the translation of the *Dhammapada* further substantiates the impression."

Reprinted now, after a generation, Babbitt's book has a topical as well as a more permanent interest. For with the war in Vietnam, Buddhists if not Buddhism itself are almost daily in the headlines in this country. One wonders, incidentally, at the connection between

119

these so-called Buddhists and the doctrines they supposedly profess when one reads of the Buddha's strong injunction against suicide and his prohibition of the very discussion of politics in the monasteries, and then thinks of priests in a Buddhist Order burning themselves in the marketplace with cameras trained upon them for very questionable political motives, setting very horrible examples that have now been followed by self-destructive teen-agers not only in Vietnam and in India but even in the United States, where the press some weeks ago reported the case of an unhappy girl of seventeen who drenched herself in gasoline and then set fire to herself! Even the most moral of doctrines is evidently not immune to perversion by its putative adherents into a caricature of itself.

That Babbitt was keenly aware of the relevance of his interest in Buddhism to the contemporary reader is clearly indicated by the striking opening of his essay on "Buddha and the Occident," which has the immediacy of an editorial in this morning's newspaper:

> The special danger of the present time would seem to be an increasing material contact between national and racial groups that remain spiritually alien. The chief obstacle to a better understanding between East and West in particular is a certain type of Occidental who is wont to assume almost unconsciously that the East has everything to learn from the West and little or nothing to give in return. One may distinguish three main forms of this assumption of superiority on the part of the Occidental: first, the assumption of racial superiority, an almost mystical faith in the preeminent virtues of the white peoples (especially Nordic blonds) as compared with the brown or yellow races; secondly, the assumption of superiority based on the achievements of physical science and the type of "progress" it promoted, a tendency to regard as a general inferiority the inferiority of the Oriental in material efficiency; thirdly, the assumption of religious superiority, less marked now than formerly, the tendency to dismiss non-Christian Asiatics en masse as "heathen," or else to recognize value in their religious beliefs, notably in Buddhism, only in so far as they conform to the pattern set by Christianity.

Babbitt was, of course, not the first American scholar to interest himself in the wisdom of the East, though few before him had pursued their studies as systematically and deeply as he did. One reason for this is that not too much was known before his time about Asiatic languages and texts. Asiatic studies, however, on a more primitive level, had long been a tradition in New England. Whatever the reason for it, there seemed to be a natural affinity between liberal Protestantism and an exotic religion that emphasized ethics almost exclusively and was largely silent on the question of a personal deity. A dissertation has been written on the subject, "Emerson and Asia," and that New England Brahmin was the fountainhead from whom the concern spread to Thoreau, Bronson Alcott, Whitman, and many others. Emerson, describing *Leaves of Grass* in one of his less charitable and sympathetic moods, called it a combination of the Bhagavadgita and the *New York Herald*. Whether this description was deserved or not, it sufficiently indicates the Asiatic coloring of his own vision of the world. Emerson's influence reached Babbitt by the diverse channels of James Russell Lowell, Charles Eliot Norton, and his own father, Edwin Babbitt. It is stamped visibly across all of his work from the Emersonian epigraph to his first book, *Literature and the American College,* to the sentence in this essay on the Buddha which reads, "A great religion is above all a great example," which sounds like a variation on the classic theme sounded in Emerson's essay *Self-Reliance*: "An institution is the lengthened shadow of a man."

To what should we attribute this Orientalism in American thought? Is its cause to be sought in the geographical position of America between Europe and Asia—the fact that this continent initially owed its discovery to the search for a trade route to India? Or is it to be sought in the filiation between New England Transcendentalism and the German Transcendental philosophy, in whose Romantic offshoot of Schopenhauer and his disciples we can trace the original stirrings of modern European interest in the spiritual insights and thought of the East?

These are large questions to which answers with any certainty probably cannot be given and on which speculation is idle. The far-reaching effect of the influence itself, however, is indisputable. By quite independent roads, the two main founders of American Humanism, Babbitt and Paul Elmer More, came to it, and from them it descended to a man like T. S. Eliot. The Oriental motif helps us to understand why *The Waste Land* concludes on the word *Shantih* from the Upanishads and why its climactic point is reached at the end of "The Fire Sermon" in Section III where we find a reconciliation between the vision of Saint Augustine, representing Western asceticism, and that of the Buddha, representing Eastern monachism.

Babbitt as a young man became so enthusiastic over his studies in Buddhism that, after his graduation from Harvard in 1889, he went abroad to the École des Hautes Études in Paris where, under the direction of Sylvain Lévi, he studied the Pali dialect of Sanskrit in which

The Dhammapada was originally composed. Of his eventual attainments intellectually in this field, we have the assurance of as sceptical a critic as T. S. Eliot who wrote in his essay entitled *The Humanism of Irving Babbitt*: "There is probably no one in England or America who understands early Buddhism better than he."

The central idea of the Buddhist ethic seems to be that restraint of every kind is a good thing, but it is desirable that restraint come from within the individual himself. Those lacking in what Babbitt terms "the inner check" will ultimately be subjected to restraint from without, which is a bitter thing to experience in contrast to self-conquest which, though difficult to achieve, is very sweet. Buddhism has much in common with other ethical systems which emphasize negative injunctions more than any positive actions. Of the ten commandments in the Decalogue, for example, it is significant that no less than seven are concerned with what men must *not* do. The daimon of Socrates, too, it should be remembered, intervened only to veto actions which were mistaken. The Golden Rule, which seems to lend encouragement to active humanitarianism and social reform rather than self-reform, is to some more persuasive perhaps in its negative form ("Thou shalt *not* do unto others . . ." etc.), as it was stated by Rabbi Hillel and by Confucius among other teachers, than it is in any other form.

It may be instructive to compare some of the Buddha's verses with moral and psychological observations to be found in literature that is more accessible to readers in the western world. For instance, sentence 186 of *The Dhammapada*: "There is no satisfying lusts even by a shower of gold-pieces; he who knows that lusts have a short taste and bring suffering in their train is wise" inevitably recalls to my own mind the 129th Sonnet of Shakespeare which begins with the line "The expense of spirit in a waste of shame is lust in action," then goes on to offer detailed evidence of this proposition, and finally ends on an ironic note in the couplet:

> All this the world well knows, yet none knows well
> To shun the heaven that leads men to this hell.

We gather from this conclusion that Shakespeare was forcibly struck with the difficulties of combining sound principles and sober practices. The Buddha, never minimizing the obstacles in the way, tends to agree with Socrates that true knowledge is redemptive to its possessor. All of our troubles stem from our ignorance, and he insists on the vital distinction between superficial knowledge resulting in casual assent and profound conviction fortified by consistent action. The world is full of people who mistake the first kind of knowledge for the second and who consequently are believers in the efficacy of glib verbal formulas mechanically mouthed. It is a safe guess that the prayer-mill must have been invented by people with just such a mentality. The Buddha has this all-too-familiar world in mind when he said in sentence 19 of *The Dhammapada*: "The slothful man even if he can recite many sacred verses, but does not act accordingly has no share in the priesthood, but is like a cowherd counting other men's kine."

The Buddha, in fact, is as stubborn in his refusal to be taken in by empty words or by ceremonial observances as any of the Hebrew Prophets or as Dante. The world in general, as Shakespeare implies, is not very strong in its ability to pattern itself on the models of morality it professes to admire, and that is why it is often deceived by the "zeal (which) lacks devotion," by mere lipservice to a cause, by hypocritical and showy "sacrifices." The Buddha, who explicitly warns his followers to be on guard against all sorts of deception not only in others but in themselves as well, would have denounced those who presume to speak in his name and yet are "workers of iniquity."

The problem of conduct, as it presented itself to both the Buddha and Babbitt, is a problem in self-perfection and self-control primarily. While this does not necessarily result in their becoming anti-social in their attitudes, it does tend to make them more or less aloof towards social concerns. Babbitt, whose own philosophy was compressed into his sentence: "In the last analysis, what a man owes to society is not his philanthropy but a good example," delightedly quotes the Buddha's rule against the discussion of politics among the monks within his Order. Too many people in the modern world, we hear him complain over and over again, escape from their immediate responsibility for mending themselves and their own lives by undertaking to meddle with the affairs of their neighbors. And whole states and societies may be afflicted with the same tendency. For Babbitt and for Buddha, perhaps as much as for Plato in *The Republic,* justice first of all consists of minding one's own business.

Only a little less important than the matter of Buddha's teaching is the manner in which he communicates it. Born a prince, the Buddha's unfailing courtesy even in the midst of a polemic against a discourteous adversary is no less notable than that of Socrates toward the rude rhetorician and Sophist Thrasymachus, whose insults he refuses to answer in kind. Many of the Buddhist Scriptures, like the Platonic Dialogues, even if they had nothing else to recommend them to us, could well serve as manuals for the instruction of youth in what it means really to be a gentleman.

The Dhammapada, it may be affirmed without fear of contradiction, is one of the few books, sacred to any religion, which is at once intelligible to the adherents of every other religion (and what is more, possibly, to the adherents of no religion at all). More than any teacher of remotely comparable influence in history, the Buddha insisted upon the universality of his message. He had nothing of the spirit of linguistic fetishism or cultural or racial exclusiveness which are encountered unfortunately among other faiths and which militate in the long run against their acceptance outside of limited areas.

It may have been this unpretentiousness which recommended Buddhism to the attention of a humanist like Babbitt who, despite his profession as a teacher of modern languages, placed little stress on the untranslatable elements which are present in every language. Babbitt is a learned author who makes no show of his learning. He rarely uses a foreign phrase to garnish his prose, as affected writers so often do, and he translates into English passages from the classics which it was clearly his prerogative to presume that his cultivated audience would understand in the original. The Buddha also was concerned mainly with his message and only very incidentally with the language in which it was delivered. The message was so clear and momentous that it was bound, he thought, to be understood no matter what the language chosen to convey it. Irving Babbitt went far to prove this true in English and for our time.

— 1965

Socrates vs. Thoreau
on Civil Disobedience

WHITMAN BEGAN HIS Preface to the 1855 edition of *Leaves of Grass* on a condescending note toward the past ("as if it were necessary to trot back, generation after generation, to the eastern records . . .") but reached the conclusion, years later, in *Democratic Vistas,* that, if faced with a choice, he would prefer to all the vast material riches of the United States the "precious minims" of a handful of literary classics, among which he named Plato. It is still unclear how much America has added to this heritage. To read, for example, Thoreau's celebrated essay "Civil Disobedience" (which has influenced profoundly Tolstoy, Gandhi, and Martin Luther King) after reading Plato's dialogue *Crito* is calculated to make one aware of the difference between a charming and even brilliant piece of rhetoric and the most ripened wisdom of mankind.

Before exploring the difference between Socrates and Thoreau, it might be well to consider what they have in common. Both are strikingly individualistic and independent of public opinion. When Crito appeals to the opinion of "the many" for support, Socrates reminds him that one should be concerned not with popularly received ideas but with those entertained by the exceptional "good men" of the world. To Crito's objection that it is prudent to heed the opinion of the masses because of the injuries they can inflict upon those who don't, Socrates responds that if "the many could do the greatest evil, they would also be able to do the greatest good," but unfortunately they can do neither. Their power is limited; their suffrage is incapable of making anyone wise or foolish, and their capacity to inflict injury is negligible since *nothing bad can happen to a good man in either life or death.* The favors of the multitude are distributed mostly by chance.

Although this Socratic view of humanity sounds "élitist" and aristocratic indeed, it seems nearly democratic and egalitarian when compared with Thoreau's austere individualism, which ancient Cynics (sometimes called "athletes of righteousness") such as Diogenes or some of their modern counterparts, like Nietzsche (who once suggested that nations are nature's roundabout efforts to create five or six great men), may sometimes match but seldom surpass. The important difference to Thoreau is not between the wise and the unwise but between those who deserve to be called men and those who don't. The multitude is composed of those whom his mentor Emerson had labelled "conformists" and Whitman called "damned simulacra." "How many men," inquires Thoreau rhetorically, "are there to a square thousand miles in this country?" and immediately answers, "Hardly one!" "The American," he tells us, "has dwindled into an Odd Fellow, who may be known by the development of his organ of gregariousness and a manifest lack of intellect and cheerful self-reliance."

Thoreau exalts the individual above the community in a manner completely un-Socratic. Thoreau's "Government" is unrelated to Socrates's State or "Laws." It may be a social necessity, but it is also of necessity an evil. It is least objectionable when it is most lax and permissive, and it would be commendable only if it resigned from its function of governing altogether, though Thoreau recognizes the proposal as visionary and Utopian. Unlike some disciples who do not hesitate to call themselves anarchists, he denies that he is a "no-government" man (as anarchists seem to have been called in his time), since he is enough of a New Englander to realize that men would have to replace the checks to their impulsive behavior which government supplies with what Irving Babbitt called "the inner check." Thoreau's individual seems to owe nothing to his "government"; on the contrary, it owes everything to him. It is a predatory, parasitical thing.

Socrates's "individual" is not the radical self-contained unit of Thoreau. He has entered, like Burke's citizen, into the compact of eternal society, which is between those who have lived before us, those who are now living, and those who will live on after us. Unlike Thoreau, whose idea that the right of the majority to impose its will on the minority stems from its physical power seems to have something in common with the sophistical view of Thrasymachus in *The Republic* which equates right with might, Socrates suggests that the laws claim our veneration because of the inestimable benefits they confer upon us.

To our parents we owe our existence, but it is the laws which have joined them together and afterwards have guided them and made provision for the education of their children. Man does not live isolated or alone in the universe of Socrates, as he does in that of Thoreau. Life in the woods was an attractive ideal to the American hermit, but it would have horrified the urbane Socrates. For Socrates, as for

Aristotle, man is a social being. He gets not merely his livelihood from the body politic to which he belongs but the very reasons for living. Socrates was not insensible to the charm of romantic scenery, but it was unable to satisfy him for long. When his young friend Phaedrus lured him once out of Athens into the surrounding countryside and invited him enthusiastically to admire the prospect before him, he acknowledged it civilly enough but complained that he could not converse with trees, no matter how beautiful they might be. Intellectual delight for Socrates derived from conversation, which was possible only in society.

It is clear that, to Socrates, polities claimed respect for their age, for the freely given consent of their citizens, and for their own obedience to long-established rules of law. The Athens which returned a verdict of death against Socrates, mistaken as it was, had all the characteristics of legitimacy. It was a weakened democracy, in the wake of an unsuccessful war, which condemned him, but it was still a legitimate state that was acting (unlike the conspiratorial oligarchy— the so-called Thirty Tyrants—that had preceded it) according to long-recognized procedures of law.

Socrates rejoices in the freedom of Athens and its reverence for law in the same spirit which characterizes the famous funeral oration of Pericles reported by Thucydides. He praises the generosity with which Athens permits her native sons the option of going and living elsewhere if for any reason they feel dissatisfied with her system of government after they have reached the age of discretion. And citizens are not merely permitted the choice of going elsewhere, they can take their property with them. The laws of Athens generously proclaim "to any Athenian . . . the liberty . . . if he does not like (these laws) when he has come of age . . . (to) go where he pleases and take his goods with him. None of (the laws) will forbid him or interfere with him. Anyone who does not like (the laws) and the city, and who wants to emigrate to a colony or to any other city, may go where he likes, retaining his property."

Loyalty to Athens was no mere mechanical reflex on the part of Socrates. He loved a city which deserved his affection. It is interesting to consider how little of the world is left even in our time of which the observations of Socrates about the permissiveness of Athens still remains true. Not that he thinks her perfect or is wholly uncritical of her. Not without reason was he suspected by the superficial of harboring sympathies for authoritarian Sparta. He sometimes sounds as if he thought the Athenian democracy the very worst of political systems, except for the others which had been tried. In a passage of *The Apology* in which he recounts his dangerous defiance of the rule of the Thirty Tyrants, he also recalls the almost fatal consequences of his dissent from the opinion of the democratic assembly in Athens on an earlier occasion. After the battle of Argunisae in 406 B.C., there was a widespread outcry against the generals involved (despite the fact that the result was a victory for the Athenians), because of the great losses of life and ships and the failure to retrieve the bodies of the dead. The result could have been described as a political lynching which, in the unseemly haste of the trial and execution of eight generals *en masse* instead of individually, violated the constitutional guarantees of Athens in the opinion of Socrates. Here is how he describes the situation in *The Apology*:

> You know, men of Athens, that I have never held any other office in the State, but I did serve on the Council. And it happened that my tribe, the Antiochis, had the Presidency at the time you decided to try the generals who had not taken up the dead after the fight at sea. You decided to try them in one body, contrary to law, as you felt afterwards. On that occasion I was the only one of the Presidents who opposed you, and told you not to break the law; and I gave my vote against it; and when the orators were ready to impeach and arrest me, and you encouraged them and hooted me, I thought then that I ought to take all risks on the side of law and justice, rather than side with you, when your decisions were unjust, through fear of imprisonment or death. That (happened) while the city was still under the democracy . . .

Socrates was not afraid of disagreeing with his fellow citizens and expressing his opinion openly and casting his vote as his conscience dictated, but this does not mean that he was arrogant enough to deny the right of his opponents to do likewise and to make their numbers prevail. A. E. Taylor, in his book *Plato: The Man and His Work,* comments on the conduct of Socrates in the following manner: "He is the one consistent 'conscientious objector' of history, because unlike most such 'objectors,' he respects the conscience of TO KOINON as well as his own." The Greek words in the text are translated by the lexicon as "the state" and are the equivalent of the Latin *res publica*.

Here is the real distinction between Socrates and Thoreau. Thoreau belongs to what Taylor describes as the usual variety of "conscientious objector." That is to say he does not regard the authority of any conscience as equal to his own, nor does he think it incumbent upon him to accept the judgment of society when it differs from his own. How different from the characteristic Socratic tone are these words from Thoreau's *Civil Disobedience*: "I do not hesitate to say that those who call themselves Abolitionists should at once effectually withdraw their support both in person and property, from the government of Massachusetts, and not wait till they constitute a majority of one, before they suffer the right to prevail through them. *I think that it is enough if they have God on their side, without waiting for that other one. Moreover, any man more right than his neighbors constitutes a majority of one already.*" (Emily Dickinson sums up this attitude in her own way when she speaks of the individual soul's "divine Majority.")

Whitman, in conversation with Traubel late in life, referred to the Abolitionists as "the red-hot fellows of those days," but the doctrine espoused by Thoreau is more incendiary and subversive than any which the Abolitionists ever propounded. "All voting," he tells us, "is a sort of gaming, like checkers or backgammon, with a slight moral tinge to it, a playing with right and wrong, with moral questions, and betting naturally accompanies it . . . Even voting *for the right* is *doing* nothing for it. It is only expressing to men feebly your desire that it should prevail. A wise man will not leave the right to the mercy of chance nor wish it to prevail through the power of the majority. . . . Only his vote can hasten the abolition of slavery who asserts his own freedom by his vote."

Though there is some Transcendental vagueness in the argument, its thrust is clear enough. It is an incitement to direct action by inflamed individuals who set their own sense of what is right above that of other men. Thoreau's approval of John Brown, whom most Americans opposed to slavery regarded as a dangerous ally and firebrand, is wholly consistent with his theoretical position in *Civil Disobedience*. Of course, Thoreau stops short of advising his hearers to take up their guns (as Brown did), but his advocacy of what has since been called "passive resistance" to the state may be little less mischievous than armed insurrection in destroying the "domestic tranquility" promised by the American Constitution and is not far removed from it. However restrained the actions of men like Gandhi, Tolstoy, Martin Luther King, and Thoreau himself may be, "passive resistance" may quickly be transformed by the masses into outright aggression to deprive others of their rights. A Pandora's box may be opened by sentences such as these in *Civil Disobedience*: "Cast your whole vote, not a strip of paper merely, but your whole influence. A minority is powerless while it conforms to the majority; it is not even a minority then; but it is irresistible when it clogs by its whole weight. If the alternative is to keep all just men in prison, or give up war and slavery, the State will not hesitate which to choose."

Refusing to pay the tax collector, according to Thoreau, would result in "a peaceable revolution, if any such be possible." But he is realistic enough to allow for more sanguinary possibilities: "Suppose blood should flow. Is there not a sort of blood shed when the conscience is wounded? Through this wound a man's real manhood and immortality flow out, and he bleeds to an everlasting death. I see this blood flowing now." On the two social questions which obsessed him — the Mexican War and slavery — he would hear of no compromise or admit the possibility that other Americans might in good conscience reach conclusions different from his own; "When a sixth of a nation which has undertaken to be the refuge of liberty are slaves, and a whole country is unjustly overrun and conquered by a foreign army, and subjected to military law, I think it is not too soon for honest men to rebel and revolutionize."

Thoreau's brand of humanitarianism is fiercely dogmatic and intolerant of any opposition. It is odd that it was left for democratic America to develop a doctrine which could be interpreted to be contemptuous of the rights of the majority. (Mill, who was concerned with the rights even of a minority of one, nowhere suggests, to my recollection, that the majority is without its rights, save those which it cares to assert by brute force.) One can understand, if not condone, a Count Tolstoy, whose country found itself under a Czar, or a Gandhi, whose country was occupied by foreigners, being tempted by the sophistries of Thoreau; it is harder to sympathize with Thoreau himself or those of his fellow citizens who sought to apply his doctrine in a country like the United States.

That the direct action advocated by Thoreau is fraught with perils hardly needs further argument in the twentieth century. Characteristically, lynchers and posses of vigilantes, mobs and those who institute inquisitions of every kind are composed of men impatient for immediate "justice" and harbor the notion that they are "more right than their neighbors." The law's delays may have driven Hamlet to distraction, but haste often kills its victims out of hand. "Deliberate speed" in the redress of grievances may be maddening to those suffering, but it is preferable to *speedy deliberation*. It was probably the requirement that capital cases be tried in a single day in ancient Athens that was responsible for the conviction of Socrates.

Concerning some of Thoreau's statements, it is difficult to say what one is expected to make of them: "Under a government which imprisons any unjustly, the true place for a just man is also in prison." It sounds well enough until we stop to think, for then it seems to lead to the conclusion inescapably that all men everywhere at all times have

belonged in jail, since there never has been nor is likely to be any
government which does not commit some injustices. Yet even Thoreau
in practice spent only a single night in jail for failure to pay his poll
tax and allowed it to be paid for him by Emerson from whom he had
gotten his oracular style of discourse. It was James Russell Lowell
who observed unkindly that Thoreau lived off the windfalls of Emerson's orchard. *Civil Disobedience* simply pushes Emerson's *Self-Reliance*
in the direction in which it was leaning. Fourteen years younger than
Emerson, Thoreau found confirmation of his own intuitions in such
sentences of Emerson's as these: "Society everywhere is in conspiracy
against the manhood of every one of its members. . . . Whoso would
be a man, must be a non-conformist."

The model of non-conformity which Emerson sets up is, ap-
propriately enough, the child, or rather, going Rousseau and the other
Romantics one better, the infant: "Infancy conforms to nobody; all
conform to it, so that one babe commonly makes four or five out of
the adults who prattle and play to it." He heartily approves those who
can hold on to this precious quality as they are growing up and com-
mends to his reader, as a further model of conduct, the example of
"the nonchalance of boys who are sure of a dinner, and would disdain as much as a lord to do or say aught to conciliate one."

The contrasts between such sentiments and those of Socrates in
the *Crito* could hardly be more striking. Socrates is so far from idealizing
childhood that it may be said that he shows a condescending if not
contemptuous attitude to it. He warns his sentimental disciple Crito
(who cannot face the thought of his master dying unjustly) that one
must not allow oneself to succumb to unreason "even if the power of
the multitude could inflict many more imprisonments, confiscations,
deaths, frightening us *like children* with hobgoblin terrors." He asks
his friend if they have really meant what they have said in the past,
or "has the argument which once was good now proved to be talk for
the sake of talking—mere *childish nonsense?*" Socrates tells Crito that
"he who is a corrupter of the laws is more than likely to be a corrupter
of *the young and foolish portion of mankind.*" Far from being a model, as
Emerson suggests, youth, according to Socrates, is a state a little like
Scotland to Samuel Johnson—very good to get away from as soon
as possible.

Not only must the wise, according to Socrates, not permit
themselves to be led by children, but their duties to their own children
enjoy no priorities among their other duties. He resists the emotional
plea of Crito that he owes it to his children to live and evade the
sentence pronounced against him. The greatest benefit we can

confer upon them is to set them a good example and to enable them to live in a city like Athens in which the laws are respected. The attitude of Socrates to the child is unflinchingly realistic. He says to Crito: "Have we, at our age, been earnestly discoursing with one another all our life long only to discover that we are no better than children." Clearly, the philosopher thinks there is a season for everything and a time "to put away childish things." True maturity is not easy to achieve, and it doesn't always accompany age.

It will hardly be denied, I suppose, that Socrates had some reason for bitterness against Athens, but it is difficult to imagine him speaking of it as Thoreau does of his America in the 1840's: "How does it become a man to behave towards this American government today? I answer that he cannot without disgrace be associated with it. I cannot for an instant recognize that political organization as my government which is the slave's government also." It is an irony of an extreme kind that Socrates who, according to Plato, died for a principle which might be denominated *civil obedience* should so often be cited by those who agree with Thoreau. Socrates explicitly denied that he was subversive of established Athenian political institutions, and his actions before his trial, at his trial, and afterwards prove that he was more attached to the ancient, orderly, constitutional structure of his city, which he had defended more than once on the field of battle, than were those democratic politicians who brought the indictment against him. They were attempting to frighten him out of the city for a variety of political motives growing out of the weakened position of the restored democracy after a period of political usurpation in the wake of a lost war. The death sentence, though it was possible under the indictment, was returned unexpectedly, largely as a result of Socrates's stubborn insistence on taking literally the language of the charge against him and his challenge to the state to show the courage to carry out its unjust sentence. Instead of choosing exile, he virtually compelled his enemies to execute him, not because he was "in opposition to the existing order," but because he was the most sincere upholder of it.

Had he resembled in any sense Voltaire's Candide, who is described by the author as "trembling like a philosopher" during a battle, there would never have been an execution and the case might never have come to trial at all. But Socrates, as we can see in Plato's *Symposium,* was not of the trembling breed of philosophers. His coolness under fire is not the least admirable of his traits. He seems to have possessed in amplest measure that faith which Whitman described as "the antiseptic of the soul." Nothing bad could happen to a good man in either life or death. Crito says to him, "I should not have liked myself, Socrates, to be in such great trouble and unrest as you are — indeed I should not. I have been watching with amazement your peaceful slumbers; and for that reason I did not awake you, because I wished to minimize the pain. I have always thought you to be of a happy disposition, but never did I see anything like the easy, tranquil manner in which you bear this calamity."

Had Thoreau been as consistent as Socrates, he would have refused to let Emerson pay the tax which he himself refused to pay, just as Socrates refused to permit the intervention of Crito on his behalf. But Thoreau found himself in jail in the first place because he had flouted the law, whereas Socrates valued the law above his own liberty. Even an admirer of Thoreau like Paul Elmer More is compelled to note: "The dangers of transcendentalism are open enough — its facile optimism and unballasted enthusiasms — dangers to the intellect chiefly. *Any one may point at the incompatibility of Thoreau's gospel with the requirements of society.*" But though this is indeed easily possible, I do not find that many writers have done so. Instead of being exposed and refuted, his sophistries have been periodically revived in times of troubles, have enlisted a formidable number of prestigious defenders, and have never contributed anything anywhere except to make confusion worse confounded. The young everywhere are particularly vulnerable, but those who are older and should know better are not immune. How else explain that his name is so often coupled with that of Socrates, as if they are both sages or as if they are both *witnesses* to the same truth? I hope to have given anyone who has ever entertained such a notion some reasons for doubting it and some incentive to examine attractive rhetoric more critically.

The cause for which Socrates laid down his life, as nearly as it can be defined, is not only the right of duly constituted authority and legitimate government to obedience by its citizens as long as it is itself obedient to its own laws, but its right to be obeyed even when it is *wrong* in its judgment. Obviously, it is a serious matter for government to be wrong even in the case of a single individual, and such a government may not continue long to govern (this is the meaning of Socrates's final warning to the court which had condemned him), but the right of legitimate governments to be wrong and the duty of the individual to obey them even in such a case are unquestionable. At any rate, Socrates, the great questioner, chose at this point to question no further.

— 1980

The Pattern of Proustian Love

IT WAS THROUGH the relationship of sexual love that Proust achieved his most penetrating insights into the powers and limitations of the mind. To systematize these insights, however, is a little like trying to marshal a series of lightning strokes in order to achieve a steady illumination over the area they are intended to reveal.

The primary step in Proust's reasoning seems to be that love is essentially a subjective phenomenon. It is created by something within a man rather than by something outside him. The Proustian affair usually takes place between a rich man (and an idle one, professionally speaking, because, as Balzac indicated, leisure is the necessary ground for allowing the pure strain of this feeling to unfold properly) and some poor opportunist. Not counting minor affairs, five major ones occupy Proust's attention — the ones between Swann and Odette, between the narrator and Gilberte, between Saint-Loup and Rachel, between Charlus and Morel, and between the narrator and Albertine. Only one of these affairs (the one between the narrator and Gilberte) involves those who are almost social equals, and yet even here the woman must be lower in social esteem since the parents of the narrator will not receive Gilberte's mother. All the other affairs are concerned with men who are rich enough to keep women, or (in the case of Charlus and Morel) with a man who keeps another man. In every case it is the woman (or the man playing the feminine role) who makes her lover suffer terribly, and in every case the cause of this suffering is the same, jealousy. If we put these facts together it is probable that in Proust suffering is what a man seeks in love, what he pays for, and why he originally falls in love. It may be useful to examine the hypothesis that such jealous love is created by the need for self-punishment in a rich, spoiled child.

The theme of the subjective nature of love, the very foundation of its psychology, is present — in disguised form, it is true — in the very opening pages of the book, in which, describing his troubled sleep, the narrator tells us: "Sometimes, too, just as Eve was created from

135

a rib of Adam, so a woman would come into existence while I was sleeping, conceived from some strain in the position of my limbs. Formed by the appetite that I was on the point of gratifying, she it was, I imagined, who offered me that gratification." It might be said that Odette, Albertine, Gilberte, Rachel and Morel are creations, in the sense that they are loved, of the minds of their lovers, just as this dream woman was a creation of the mind of the sleeper. They are all eventually proved as accidental and as subjective as she is.

Perhaps this oblique and veiled way of stating the theme is even more satisfactory to the imagination of the reader than a more explicit statement of it: "I had guessed long ago in the Champs-Elysées, and had since established to my own satisfaction, that when we are in love with a woman we simply project into her a state of our own soul, that the important thing is, therefore, not the worth of the woman, but the depth of the state; and the emotions which a young girl of no kind of distinction arouses in us can enable us to bring to the surface of our consciousness some of the most intimate parts of our being."

Proust has an ambiguous attitude toward this power of transformation possessed by the mind — admiration of the enchanter and contempt for the objects, and the progress in Proust, if there is any, is the same as the one we find in *Don Quixote,* from enchantment to disenchantment. That is why Proust's pages are so filled with unhappiness, for happiness, as Swift informs us, is "a perpetual possession of being well deceived," and none of Proust's people are so permanently possessed. Sooner or later, like Cervantes's hero, they awaken from their dreams to the accompaniment of shame and torment. Proust does take a certain pride in the lover's poetic ability, which might be compared to Rimbaud's voluntary derangement of his senses so that he should be able to see a romantic mosque in place of an ordinary prosaic brick factory. This pride is present, for example, in Proust's pointed comment on the look of disillusion so plainly printed on Saint-Loup's face when the narrator shows him the photograph of his mistress: "Let us leave pretty women to men devoid of imagination."

It is the subjective nature of love, its growth in the soil of mind alone rather than in any external, material realities, that makes its bodily realization the least important of its phases. When Albertine leaves the narrator, it is not as a woman that he regrets her. She would not have been very dangerous to his tranquility if he had been able to think of her physically, because he knows intellectually that she is not at all remarkable in that way. She brings anguish with her because she is an image of frustration.

It is difficult to detach the idea of love from that of physical beauty;

the connection of the two is a prejudice very early ingrained into our minds. It is as painful to part with this prejudice as to part with our pride. In Proust, certainly, good looks have no causal connection with the feeling of love. Instead, it is *anxiety* that is central. Perhaps that is why famous lovers of history (like Cleopatra whose beauty Plutarch specifically denies, emphasizing instead the charm of her voice!) have not been necessarily the beauties but the *fugitives*. That is, those who exploit our anxieties and terrors by seeming to threaten constantly to take flight from us. If personality in general, according to Proust, is unstable, it is the most unstable personalities that seem to inspire the most fervent attachments. Why this should be so, I shall try presently to deduce from Proust's analysis, but that it is indeed so, he leaves little room for doubt: "Generally speaking, love has not as its object a human body, except when an emotion, the fear of losing it, the uncertainty of finding it again have been infused into it. This sort of anxiety has a great affinity for bodies. It adds to them a quality which surpasses beauty even; which is one of the reasons why we see men who are indifferent to the most beautiful women fall passionately in love with others who appear to us to be ugly."

It is this hallucinatory quality of love which makes us see things as no one in his right senses would see them, that makes Proust refer to love continually as a disease, a compulsion, a poison. Whether a given person who has caught it ever recovers from it depends on his reserves or resistance, the strength of his mental constitution, and the seriousness of the original infection. There is no way of saying in advance whether the thing is going to be fatal or not. Once the recovery is complete, however, the sufferer (which is to say, etymologically, the *passionate* man) can see the world once again in the same light as everybody else, and then it must be clear to him that it was something in himself which he called his love and not something outside. So after Swann expends his time, his fortune, and very nearly his life itself in his vain (and necessarily vain, for love cannot be compelled — the effort to compel it only alienates it still further) pursuit of Odette, he, who had compared her to a Botticellian masterpiece, who would have said in the manner of the elders of Troy when they beheld Helen: "All our misfortunes are not worth a single glance of her eyes," who had desired death as a relief from the intolerable pain of his unrequited love, suddenly, luckily, unexpectedly, reaches the opposite shore of sanity and is able to look back in wonder at the illusion which had nearly undone him. Then there follows the famous coda of the chapter called "Swann in Love," which recounts his reawakening to reality, accomplished ironically through the agency of a dream! ". . . he saw

once again as he had felt them close beside him Odette's pallid com-
plexion, her too thin cheeks, her drawn features, her tired eyes, all
the things which — in the course of those successive bursts of affection
which had made of his enduring love for Odette a long oblivion of
the first impression he had formed of her — he had ceased to observe
after the first few days of intimacy . . . and he cried out in his heart:
'To think that I have wasted years of my life, that I have longed for
death, that the greatest love that I have ever known has been for a
woman who did not please me, who was not in my style!"

If we turn now to the other half of the team of love, the part
represented by Odette, Rachel, Gilberte, Albertine and Morel, we
find that they are the ones who let themselves be loved. They are the
carriers of the disease but are not themselves affected by it. They see
the world only too clearly to mistake their dreams for reality. They
are hardheaded Sanchos, who look for their rewards in the governor-
ship of some island promised them by their crazy masters, except that,
being shrewder than Sancho was, they choose to follow men who
already possess islands instead of one who is only planning to conquer them. The connections which Proust traces between love and
the opportunity to enter society, to acquire money, to advance one's
career, and in general to gain material advantage, would appear to
be extremely cynical, were it not for the fact that the circumstantial
details which he supplies show very clearly that he knows what he
is talking about.

To Proust, there seems no possibility for the development of all
the potentialities of love which shall illustrate his laws, where there
is an absence of money, position, or other advantages. In the latter
case, the affair is doomed even before its growth. Where there is no
leisure, there may be a simulacrum of romantic love, or simple sex,
but not love in the involved, fully developed Proustian sense. Love
is a luxury, and only sex is a necessity, consequently while every one
can enjoy the latter, only a few can afford the former. Quite seriously, Proust quotes the aphorism of La Bruyère: "It is a mistake to fall
in love without an ample fortune." That is a mistake which Proust's
characters never make.

All the lovers in Proust are conscious of the advantage which is
gained for them by their titles or their wealth. And they are continually
uneasy about the sufficiency or continuation of these advantages. We
find Saint-Loup looking forward to a rich though loveless marriage
in order that he might be able to afford keeping his mistress Rachel.
For though he drugs his pain occasionally with the optimistic self-
assurance that it is really himself and not his money she loves, he is

really aware that his little friend suffers him "only on account of his money, and that on the day when she had nothing more to expect from him, she would make haste to leave him." Nor does the narrator show any more confidence about his relations with Albertine when he says: "Pecuniary interest alone could attach a woman to me."

It is to be noted, however, that Proustian love is never inspired by outright prostitutes. Even when the woman has sold herself in the past for a definite low sum (as is the case with Rachel), that fact is not known to her great lover, though it may be known to all his friends. Saint-Loup never finds out about Rachel, nor does Swann about Odette (until it is too late for them to be interested), because as Proust shows us (and it is one of his most excellent observations), around every lover there is woven necessarily a conspiracy of silence, either by the considerateness of people towards him or their cruelty. If it is obvious to the reader that Swann, Saint-Loup and the rest are the purchasers of the favors they receive, they have nevertheless been convinced by a very artful process that they are quite exceptional and that their virtuous mistresses have been seduced and corrupted by them. If this sounds funny, it is because it actually is funny, though the dupe is not expected to appreciate the joke. Proust thinks that the failure of prostitutes to inspire love is due to the fact that there must always be "a risk of impossibility" standing between ourselves and our object to lend its possession savor. Therefore, he concludes, difficult women alone are interesting, and love is always born of uncertainty. Difficult women but not impossible ones. Completely virtuous women are without power to inspire love either. When the narrator is repelled by Albertine at Balbec and draws the erroneous conclusion that she is impossible to seduce, his interests in her cools immediately. It is only those women who are doubtful in their morals who are capable of exercising a fatal attraction upon men. Women who seem to be wavering in their allegiance to virtue without being yet committed to vice; women who *this time alone* seem capable of succumbing to the lure of money or position but are not known to have yielded to this weakness before.

The connections between love and guilt are both subtle and manifold. Essentially it is a nameless guilt of which the sufferings caused by jealousy are the expiation. Swann's grief over his love and his need continually to speak of it to anybody who will listen is compared by Proust to the murderer's need to confess. This "figure of speech" is far from accidental. It is not *we* who seek love, but the albatrosses that hang round our necks. The proof of the morality of Proust's vision of the world, if any were needed (and at least some of his critics like Mauriac and Fernandez have felt that it was), is that pain seems to him a retribution — ultimately, his language may suggest, of original sin. The merit of love is that when its tortures become unbearably excruciating, they may lead us to a re-examination of our festering consciences. A man unfortunate enough to fall into the net of a woman like Odette must ask himself at some point — what did I ever do to deserve this? The answer that Proust gives to this question is "Plenty!" In that tremendous scene which closes the volume *Cities of the Plain,* in which Albertine finally secures her death grip on the heart of the narrator, by the perfectly silly accident of her lying claim to intimacy with Vinteuil's daughter (whose perversion the narrator is aware of but Albertine is not), he reveals under the shock of his despair the burden of guilt which he had carried in his heart but concealed from himself for so long. His torments then appear to him ". . . as a punishment, as a retribution (who can tell?) for my having allowed my grandmother to die, perhaps, rising up suddenly from the black night in which it seemed forever buried, and striking, like an Avenger, in order to inaugurate for me a novel, terrible, and merited existence, perhaps also to make dazzlingly clear to my eyes the fatal consequences which evil actions indefinitely engender, not only for those who have committed them, but for those who have done no more, have thought that they were doing no more than look on at a curious and entertaining spectacle, like myself, alas, on that afternoon long ago at Montjouvain, concealed behind a bush where (as when I complacently listened to an account of Swann's love affair), I had perilously allowed to expand within myself the fatal road, destined to cause me suffering, of knowledge."

So here, many volumes later, we have the logical conclusion of that Biblical image in the opening pages in which a woman was created by the strain in a sleeper's limbs "just as Eve was created from a rib of Adam." Woman the cause of man's transgression originally is also the instrument with which he is punished.

We instinctively love what will make us suffer. "We are wrong in speaking of a bad choice in love," says Proust, "since whenever there is a choice it can only be bad." In another place he says: "It is human to seek out what hurts us." And when we consider all the positive *good* that accrues to us through the medium of our sufferings, we conclude by being grateful for it and we see that we have chosen right after all. ". . . A woman is of greater service to our life if she is in it, instead of being an element of happiness, an instrument of sorrow, and there is not a woman in the world the possession of whom is as precious as that of the truths she reveals to us by making us suffer."

Suffering is so valuable to Proust because, without it, he thinks we must always remain strangers to ourselves. "How much further," he exclaims at one point, "does anguish penetrate in psychology than psychology itself!" By the second term, we are to understand cold intellectual self-analysis. The innermost nature of life for Proust as for Schopenhauer is something much more akin to feeling than it is to reason—consequently thought can work best when aroused by the keenest of all feelings which is pain. Schopenhauer says of death that it is the muse of all philosophy, and Proust makes of frustrated love the inspiration of all art. From his most youthful works to his latest ones, an idea which recurs in Proust is that suffering is what inspires us (that is to say the best of us, for the others are hardened and made more callous in proportion to their sufferings) with feelings of sympathy for other men; without such sympathy there can be no understanding or communication between men and therefore no art either.

The need for suffering which it fulfills is the reason why love has a basic affinity for attaching itself to cruel people. The lover in Proust always has "an excess of good nature," and the loved one "an excess of malice." Therefore we have a very wide latitude of choice, for Proust thinks that people in general tend to be cruel—and cowardly at the same time. One of his most striking aphorisms about human nature is that while we all enjoy tormenting others, we hesitate to put ourselves clearly in the wrong by killing them outright. Morel, Rachel, Gilberte, and Odette are displayed to us in a great variety of postures denoting willful torture, sometimes of their unfortunate lovers, sometimes of other innocents. The Rachel who arranges with her coterie to hiss a rival actress off the stage is the same Rachel who taunts Saint-Loup. Morel is exhibited in perhaps the greatest variety of such actions. His public rebuff of his patron Charlus, after the concert which the latter has arranged to introduce him to fashionable society, is one of the most painful scenes in literature. As for Gilberte, she is cruel not only to Marcel but to her own father as well. And in this respect, she shows herself worthy of her mother Odette, the depths of whose inconceivable depravity are sounded by Swann when he suspects her of being capable of hiding a lover in their room in order to inflame the senses of the latter or simply to torture him by allowing him to witness her lovemaking with Swann. Albertine seems to the narrator the heaven-sent instrument of his castigation—he speaks of "the contrary, inflexible will of Albertine, upon which no pressure had had any effect." Such are the ideal objects of love because sensitive men, according to Proust, "need to suffer."

In one passage, which is about no character in the book in

particular but rather deals in the abstract with those qualities of woman which are most attractive, Proust sums up his impressions in phrases which show unmistakably, by the isolation of certain traits of physiognomy and posture, that it is the external features which seem best to denote an inward coldness and cruelty or at least lack of sympathy which prove compelling—I mean such expressions as "haughty calm," "indifferent," "the proud girl," "the beauty of stern eyes."

Proustian love is a passion in which the consent of the sufferer is necessary—at least at first; after that, it acts like the spring of a trap which has been released. *If the femme fatale did not exist, the romantic would have to invent her, for she corresponds to his need for suffering, and necessity is the mother of invention.* In the respect that consent is necessary at the beginning, love is like hypnosis, because no one can be hypnotized against his will, nor be made to do anything while in that state which runs counter to his basic character formation. So, no one who is not at least potentially a criminal to begin with can be made to commit a crime by suggestion. But though the consent of the patient is necessary at first in order to induce the state (of either love or hypnosis) once the state is fully established and confirmed, one may be influenced to do many painful things, and the process of awakening, unless managed very skillfully by a physician (but in love the cause is not a physician—it is a disease), may be very difficult and disturbing. This matter of consent and foreknowledge of the passion of love before it becomes fixed is very important. It indicates that love is something which, in spite of all its troubles, is sought as an expiation of some anterior guilt, which would be even more serious to face—just as some types of mental illness can apparently be arrested only by the artificial stimulation of such high fevers as are themselves eventually dangerous to life. We are constantly forced, like Ulysses, to choose between evils, and if we choose love, it must be because unconsciously we regard it as the lesser one in comparison with some other dread, the very name of which we suppress from our minds, though it may perhaps occasionally be brought to the surface by a skillful analyst. Charlus makes the brilliant observation at one point that homosexuality is probably a disease which prevents a man from suffering an even more dangerous one.

Swann had been cautious with his heart before he met Odette. He had stayed within easy reach of shore. He had never given himself deeply to any of his numerous female friends, and he had never lost that mastery of himself which, so long as it is retained, keeps him from being a lover in the Proustian sense—that is to say helplessly, compulsively, perhaps even convulsively. In general, Swann is a man whose awakenings to the fundamental realities about himself come very late — that is true not only of his great love for Odette but of his discovery of the importance of his Jewish identity under the impact of the Dreyfus Case. The motivations which make him *consent* to become involved with Odette as he had successfully avoided becoming involved with anyone before that are multiple — curiosity about the life which lovers lead of which he had read and heard and dreamt so much though he had not the courage to try it (in which caution he was well-advised, it seems, for it very nearly costs him his life when he does experience it), respect for the nobility of self-sacrifice in love, and finally his own lack of fulfillment as an artist which he associated with his lack of the inspiration of love. Swann proves that love is the most literary of emotions. Love, which is the subject of so much of the world's art, is itself stimulated by works of art. La Rochefoucauld observes that many a man would never have fallen in love had he not read about it first.

But this is not to say, as I have tried to indicate, that love does not fulfill a subjectively compelling necessity. Proust speaks of "our need of a great love," by which he means, as I understand him, a love not lightly taken or trivial, but profound and spiritually exhausting. Only when love, like an enraged bull, comes within an ace of killing you (sometimes, of course, it does actually gore its victim to death) can you be sure that it is the real thing, the salutary terror which allays the memory of all your nameless guilt. "Slight" love affairs in Proust's pages serve as relaxations between more serious ones. The source of much tragedy in the world and almost all in Proust is that the nature of things makes it seem inevitable that there should be very few beings who correspond to "our need of a great love" and only too many to take advantage of it. Proust makes it clear in reference to the narrator, by the use which he makes of the Mme. de Stermaria episode, that at a given moment of his life, a man is simply ready for his great love affair. The object of his feeling is certainly of secondary importance if not entirely accidental. He is determined by his whole past to let himself fall into the death lock of love.

Love is the ultimate test of life in Proust. The analogy which he makes of it with war has been used many times before, but it is given new force by him. Like war, it is a situation in which the control of our destiny is committed into the hands of another. Like war, love is a test from which we may not return alive (though our friends do not always notice that they are really conversing with our ghosts!). Like war, too, it terrifies and thrills us simultaneously with a feeling of our own insignificance and helplessness. There seems to be a carnal attraction to danger. That all of the greatest love affairs of literature and history — Anthony and Cleopatra, Paolo and Francesca, Héloïse and Abélard, Tristan and Isolde, Romeo and Juliet, Launcelot and Guinevere, Hero and Leander, Dido and Aeneas — seem to have been in some way illicit or at least surrounded by dangers and pitfalls is not just a coincidence.

It is characteristic of Proust's lovers that they know *in advance* the path that their love is bound to follow *or think they do*. Thus, from the moment that he is inextricably taken in the toils of Albertine, the narrator compares his own situation with that of Swann which he had once heard about. Yet this intellectual knowledge is without visible effect upon his actions. The pattern which all the different affairs follow is their nonreciprocity: "I felt even then that in a love which is not reciprocated — I might as well say in love, for there are people for whom there is no such thing as reciprocated love. . . ." We may add here that the people for whom there is no such thing as reciprocated love are all the people in Proust, because, if there are any others, he either did not observe them or describe them, though his careful phrasing occasionally leaves room for the possibility that somewhere they may actually exist.

The initial condition of love, then, is the expectant, perhaps even eager condition of the organism that awaits it (if I use such scientific verbiage, it is because Proust's clinical treatment of the subject suggests it). The immediate cause of love, in the presence of this weakened and assenting state, is, as I have said, less than nothing in comparison with the vast uproar and turmoil which follows. Proust compares the immediate cause of love to "an insignificant bacillus" which is capable of making the proudest men die. Charlus says very well that it is not whom or what one loves that matters, but the fact of loving itself.

I have spoken of the cruelty of those who cause the most lasting passions in Proust. This is not always intentional cruelty, though it can be, but merely thoughtlessness, carelessness, or stupidity. The thoughtlessness of Odette is invaluable to her in bringing about some of Swann's most violent paroxyms. He clearly realizes her lack of intelligence. In fact, we might put the Proustian thought in this way, exaggerating his pessimism a bit perhaps but not being basically unfair to him — *the more moral worth a person is possessed of, the more sensitive he is, the more intelligent and considerate, the less are his chances of inspiring that great love which we all need as an expiation.* The more worthless the object of love the better, for in that case we are bound to suffer more excruciatingly, and that suffering is what we really seek to find, without clearly knowing it from the beginning, or admitting it to ourselves eventually perhaps. A sensitive, moral, intelligent being would hesitate, after all, to involve us in so tormenting and hopeless a situation, and, if we became involved in spite of such care, once he realized what was happening, he would do his best to extricate us and to assuage the pain he had unwittingly caused. A good, strong, wise person is therefore constitutionally unfitted for the work which is left for those insignificant bacilli, Odette, Rachel, Gilberte, Albertine, and Morel.

Jealousy is the inseparable shadow of love. And just as a man or any material body which casts no shadow would be impalpable or unreal, so Proust doubts the existence of any love which finds no counterpart in jealousy. There seems to be an absolutely necessary place for jealousy in the pattern of love, and it seems very often that we are jealous *not* because we are in love, but that we are in love in order that we might be jealous.

The women in Proust who are the most successful in arousing love are those who recognize instinctively its connection with the personal insecurity and anxiety of the lover. Albertine knows how to exploit the narrator's jealousy, just as Odette had exploited Swann's. In their own persons, these women bore their lovers; what gives them their power is the desire which they arouse in others. Women enchain us in proportion to the suffering they cause. The initial shock of anxiety is sudden in its onset and knocks down the surprised lover before he really knows what is happening. He had not known himself so weak till that moment. Swann had never even kissed Odette before the evening of his fall, when he missed her from her accustomed place at the Verdurins'. Without knowing why he is rendered frantic and "ransacks" the streets of Paris for the missing Odette until by some ill chance (or "retribution," as Proust might put it) he finds her again. He is led to his fate as blindly as Oedipus once travelled the road from Corinth to Thebes. It is at this point of the story that Proust writes one of his most amazingly suggestive paragraphs on the origin and mystery of love:

> Among all the methods by which love is brought into being, among all the agents which disseminate that blessed bane, there are few so efficacious as the great gust of agitation which, now and then, sweeps over the human spirit. For then the creature in whose company we are seeking amusement at the moment, her lot is cast, her fate and ours decided, that is the creature whom we shall henceforward love. It is not necessary that she should have pleased us up till then, any more, or even as much as others. All that is necessary

is that our taste for her should become exclusive. And that condition is fulfilled as soon as — for the pleasure which we were on the point of enjoying in her charming company is abruptly substituted an anxious, torturing desire, which the laws of civilized society make it impossible to satisfy and difficult to assuage — the insensate, agonizing desire to possess her.

If the power of women over men, as Proust illustrates this truth in a hundred variations (so that his demonstration gradually assumes the rigor of mathematics), grows with each pang of suffering they cause, that is because, like Baudelaire and Poe, Proust thinks that in human nature itself there lurks some "demon of perversity." It is this demon of perversity which explains why the most senseless and harmful habits in human life are also the hardest ones to shake off. The human condition for Proust is one of futility. The least unkind thing he has to say about sexual love is that it is "a sedative." It drugs momentarily the saddest and silliest element in human nature, our vanity, and it temporarily appeases our insatiable egos by supplying us with an illusory, imaginative triumph "over countless rivals."

We can see how this psychological structure is related to his conception of the human personality with its discontinuities, its innumerable fissures, its general instability and changeableness, its lightning shifts of mood and key. Whoever puts his reliance upon human beings composed of such fragmentary elements steps upon a spiritual quicksand. Since the relationship of sexual love implies the heaviest reliance upon the personality and will of other people, it is liable to sink deepest into the quagmire. The safest course for a human being sentenced to this world (unless he is lucky or blessed enough to enjoy divine love which seems to mitigate the punishment somewhat) is to steer alone. Proust at the end rejects friendship and society along with love. Only art survives his bitter criticism, and art, as we remember from the well-known passage on the death of the novelist Bergotte, is a reminder of the possible, not the necessary existence of another and better world than the one we are aware of through our senses.

If, as Proust reiterates, we must remain in perpetual ignorance even of ourselves and our feelings, just as the kaleidoscope is ignorant of the pattern which will turn up after the next shake, we are condemned to an even darker and more abysmal ignorance of our mysteriously moving neighbors in life. One reason that love is so torturing is that the more we are interested in other people the less, it seems, we can know about them. It is when we no longer care that the truth, so carefully concealed when we would have given our lives for it, suddenly floats like scum to the surface. It is only years after the end of his affair with Gilberte that her double life at the time Marcel loved her becomes known to him. It is not Swann who learns from Charlus that she is a troublesome gay lady whom he had once gotten rid of. And it is only after Marcel is hopelessly enmeshed with Albertine that he learns from her that his first and fatal step was taken because she had lied to him about her acquaintanceship with Mlle. Vinteuil.

Nor does thinking things through seem to help any. There are an infinite number of hypotheses about the intentions of other people. I once heard the greatest chess player in the world define life as the game at which we are all duffers. The sources of all the greatest events in life like the sources of great rivers, says Proust, remain hidden from us and are sought in vain. We can trace them step by step, but one more step always remains possible after the latest discovery we have made. It is an inflexible law that, as one of the subdivisions of that vast ignorance of things which Socrates, Ecclesiastes, and the wisest men of all times and nations have recognized as the ultimate destiny of humanity, we must also remain ignorant of those whom we love best.

—1951

On Céline Once More

"Maybe Céline will be the only one of us who endures . . ."
—*Jean-Paul Sartre*

MY FEELING ABOUT the historical and literary importance of Céline's letters to me was indicated as early as 1948 when, before leaving for Europe with the intention of visiting him in Denmark, I deposited his letters to me in a safe-deposit box in a bank in Chicago with instructions to my wife, in the event that I did not return, to explore the possibility of publishing them. More than a decade later, most of them were purchased from me by an agent for the Humanities Research Center of the University of Texas in Austin for its remarkable collection of twentieth-century manuscripts. What interested me was the assurance that they would be preserved for the use of scholars and critics, and there is little in the extensive scholarship and criticism of Céline that has not benefited from them. A selection of them has been translated and published by the University of Texas in its *Quarterly*, and the unabridged French texts of the letters have been published several times in Paris in periodical as well as in book form. I handed over more than eighty letters to the University but held back for my own use a dozen or so and also kept the copies of most of my letters to Céline.

I had no plans at the beginning to do more than correspond with Céline; it was he who began to try to persuade me to come to Denmark to see him. Though I was not eager to do so, I had no objections either, apart from the general inertia that I shared with Italo Svevo's character Zeno, who "always found it as difficult to start when he was at rest as to stop once he was in motion." My curiosity could be satisfied intellectually by reading something that had been written. I loved to travel, not geographically, but in what Keats has beautifully called "the realms of gold," disclosed to our imaginations by literature and history.

One day I mentioned in one of my letters a dream I had had in which I was on my way by boat to see him in Europe. I said jokingly

149

that since dreams were supposed to represent wish-fulfillments, he ought not to doubt my deep desire to visit him even if there were practical difficulties standing in the way. He replied immediately that it was necessary not only to dream but to translate the dream into reality, and he was soon full of ingenious suggestions as to how this might be managed. He thought, for example, that I might launch an inquiry as to the role played by various writers during the war. I might interview not only himself on this delicate subject but André Malraux, Jean-Paul Sartre, André Gide, and others. He even suggested I might propose an inquiry that would be backed by some American rabbis, and to back this up he sent me a newspaper clipping in which it was reported that a prominent American rabbi had said that the great need, now that the war was over, was for the reconciliation of former enemies with each other.

Meanwhile, Céline had made me his unpaid representative in dealing with James Laughlin and New Directions, which was preparing to put his out-of-print works back in print. The first of these, for which I wrote an introduction, was *Death on the Installment Plan*. I should have preferred that the initial invitation to readers to rediscover Céline would be *Journey to the End of the Night,* but perhaps because this had been too recent a sensational success and needed no rediscovery, Laughlin chose to lead off with *Death*. In fact, the two books might be considered halves of a single creatively autobiographical fiction with the chronological order reversed—*Journey* covers the author's experience from the age of eighteen to his middle thirties (the book was published in Céline's thirty-eighth year and had been started four years before), while *Death on the Installment Plan* is concerned in the main with the writer's childhood, adolescence, and young manhood until he decides, on the day he becomes eligible for military service at the age of eighteen, to exchange his "idyllic" life before the First World War (which comes to a climax in a brutal physical battle between Ferdinand and his father, whom he nearly kills) for the regimentation of the army.

Death on the Installment Plan is not nearly as aphoristic as *Journey to the End of the Night*. It is not in nearly so much of a hurry to deliver its author's cynical judgments on everything under the sun in the modern world: imperialism, industrialism, America, colonialism, the bourgeoisie, medicine, research, psychiatry, women, and so on. *Death on the Installment Plan* is less naturalistic in its literary method than *Journey* had been, though *Journey*, under a thin veneer of realism, is a visionary work filled with delirious hallucinations, a Dostoyevskian "Double," and such anachronistic decor as that great slave-propelled sixteenth-century "galley" on which Ferdinand makes his journey from the African "heart of darkness" to the American "air-conditioned nightmare." Céline, in his creative work, rarely alludes to his own erudition and culture (which are clearly evident in his correspondence with me), yet in *Journey* he had spoken knowledgeably, though *en passant*, about Marcel Proust and had even dared risk a bout of satirical sword-play with the great essayist Montaigne himself (whom, in his "pamphlets," he was to treat as slightly *tainted* with Jewishness). In *Death on the Installment Plan*, his depiction of frenzy is more daring and surrealistic than it is in *Journey*, his Rabelaisian vocabulary and explicit pornographic use of sexual materials (as in the wildly humorous scene in which Madame Gorloge seduces young Ferdinand) are so extreme that the work was published initially in expurgated form for fear of the police. The excisions were not restored until the Pléiade edition almost thirty years later.

Céline's most striking artistic success in *Death on the Installment Plan* is his portrayal of the inventor, confidence man, writer-publisher, trickster, picaro, impresario, and ignoble *Don Quixote*, whom he calls Courtial des Pereires. In his letters to me, Céline identified a model for Pereires in a writer and inventor named Henri de Graffigny, whose Jules Verne-like romances, scientific pamphlets, and books he assured me were still on sale in stalls on the Left Bank in Paris. There is a Jewish overtone in the name *Pereires* as well a significant resemblance between it and the name *Giacobbo Rodriguez Pereire* (or *Pereiro*) who is identified by the Encyclopaedia Britannica as a Spaniard born in Estremadura in 1715, who died in Paris in 1780. Pereire is described by the encyclopedia as the inventor of deaf-mute language, who had fallen in love with a girl who had been dumb from birth "and devoted himself to discovering a method of imparting speech to deaf-mutes. He devised a sign alphabet for the use of one hand." These little-known facts become relevant to the reader of *Death on the Installment Plan* not only because Céline's character Courtial des Pereires is an inventor but also because his hero Ferdinand, when he is sent off to an English boarding school early in the novel, out of sheer disgust with the world around him and especially his own family, renounces his powers of speech and "clams up" so completely that he gives to others the impression of being a deaf-mute.

Courtial des Pereires is a charlatan on a truly magnificent and heroic scale, for whom the reader, who begins by laughing contemptuously at him, learns eventually to feel such real affection that his suicide proves heartbreaking. It may not be as emotionally overpowering as the ending of *The Brothers Karamazov*, but what is? Céline may

not have succeeded in creating the kind of book Kafka had in mind
when he said that the truly necessary work is "like an axe for the frozen
sea within us." Not many books measure up to such a criterion. Yet
Céline has constructed a character in whom it is possible for a reader
to believe enough to be deeply moved by his self-destruction. Gide
thought that the character of Courtial was drawn somewhat conven-
tionally. That is not how I see it. To me he seems three-dimensional,
objective, and life-like in the sense that his actions and words are always
surprising, unexpected, and yet somehow consistent. Above all, the
reader can hear Courtial talk. He is the greatest of Céline's talkers,
outside of the narrator Ferdinand himself, who, after the recovery
of his powers of speech, develops a truly astounding verbal virtuosity
that enables him to mimic the effects of Courtial and to raise them
to a higher power, so that he is able to create the equivalent of a
frightening mask, which serves all his needs of expression without in-
voking such an old-fashioned concept as "sincerity." To my mind,
Courtial des Pereires is a triumph of character creation that, if not
quite on a level with Cervantes' immortal Quixote, requires no apology
for being mentioned in the same breath with him. Céline, who
respected few writers who were fashionable, never spoke of Cervantes
save with reverence. Admiring the Spaniard's inventive power, he also
identified with him as a soldier who had been crippled in battle and
who exposed the vanity and falsehood of the romancers of his time.
Céline's aspiration was to make other writers of his time seem as ob-
solete as Cervantes had once done. If he did not succeed entirely in
this, it can hardly be said that he failed either. Certainly, his effect
on myself and on numbers of other readers can only be described as
obsessive during a period of our lives in which his visions seemed the
most accurate rendering of the fantastic, maddening world in which
we found ourselves.

Courtial des Pereires is an inventor himself, but his real vocation is that of impresario for the inventions of others, whom he
unhesitatingly cheats. His clientele is that large gaping public (P. T.
Barnum's eternal "suckers") upon whom he tirelessly imposes. Under
his tutelage, young Ferdinand, who plays the role of both squire and
sorcerer's apprentice, discovers the world of gullibility. Eventually,
it seems as if this world contains us all, including the master exploiter
himself, Courtial. There is an immense horde of would-be inventors
in the world, all waiting patiently (or else pushing and shoving) to
have their unique genius discovered. Everyone in the world has his
particular story to tell; everyone has his little imaginary sailboat fitted
out with "all his little lies," hoping "to catch the wind." The "wind,"

of course, is that of popular favor and acceptance from that greater mass of "suckers" incapable of inventions of their own and deriving a kind of vicarious satisfaction from the lies of the inventors.

But a man like Courtial does not only lie to others; he is taken in by his own myths as well. He really believes in the Progress he preaches; he really believes in a Jules Verne-like scientific and technological future, to which it is the height of his ambition to make a contribution. But while waiting for this marvelous Utopian future, he acts abominably to his wife and to those foolish enough to place their trust in him. In the end, however, he is hoist on his own petard. Despite all his manifold skills, knowledge (really encyclopedic), shrewdness, and lack of compunction, his ill-conceived, hare-brained schemes collapse. His overactive imagination makes him overextend himself, and it is his belated recognition of this that causes him to destroy himself. In many ways, he is emblematic of the overweening and even insane ambitions of modern engineering and technology. There is one thing he does not fail at, and that is to wind himself up to a pitch of gaseous idealism that enables him to soar effortlessly above the clouds in defiance of the forces of gravity and common sense. It is symbolically in keeping with the picture of Courtial that one of his main props should be a gas-filled balloon with which he travels around the French countryside, putting on exhibitions designed to attract the attention of the yokels. It is the verbal pyrotechnics of Courtial that inspire Ferdinand, so recently dumb, not only to imitate the effects of his "boss" but also, by entering a heightened state of nervous delirium, to attain levels of hyperbole that surpass him. In this respect, Courtial becomes the benefactor and instructor of Ferdinand. He learns through him how to deal with, impress, and communicate with a world that had hitherto completely baffled him. Courtial des Pereires becomes a sort of substitute father for Ferdinand, whose own pigheaded father has proved so unsatisfactory. When Courtial commits suicide and Ferdinand comes to blows with his own father and reaches an absolute impasse with him, it is Ferdinand's uncle who takes over temporarily from his immediate family and gives him shelter until the age at which he is able to escape into the prison of army service, which is not an illogical way out for him.

Courtial des Pereires, like Ferdinand Bardamu in *Journey to the End of the Night,* seems to feel that the choice given us by life is between "dying and lying"; coming to the end of his tether of lies, he manages, unlike Ferdinand, to screw his courage to the sticking point and blow his brains out. In that sense, he becomes something of an inspiring example (like Werther), and his role in *Death on the*

Installment Plan is parallel to that of Léon Robinson in *Journey*, who does not kill himself but manages to goad his rejected fiancée, Madelon, into shooting him. All of these characters, not to speak of the author himself, remind one of a passage in Cervantes in which it is said of Don Quixote that he impresses Don Diego de Miranda "as being a crazy sane man and an insane one on the verge of sanity." That is close to the impression made on me by Céline himself when I met him in Denmark, and it is a paradox I tried to convey in *The Crippled Giant*. I confess to thinking on occasion that I might say of Céline what Cervantes said of his character: "For me alone Don Quixote was born and I for him."

But why did I go to see Céline? Elementary as this question seems, it has to be asked over and over again. For a long time, I have been asked it by others. Now I ask it of myself. The deepest roots of my attachment to Céline may be impossible to trace. Jewish self-hatred? If this glib phrase is not simply a put-down, what does it really mean? There are questions that, like the famous ones raised by Sir Thomas Browne (what songs the Sirens sang or what name Achilles assumed among women), may not be beyond all conjecture but seem outside the range of profitable speculation. Nowadays, when I look again at *Journey to the End of the Night* in French or in English, it isn't easy to recapture the pristine enthusiasm it inspired in me forty years ago. Yet it is still possible to realize how many admirable things there are in it from a literary point of view: its sheer cleverness, its spontaneity, its freedom from cant and inhibition, its verve and verbal skill. The original French text is, of course, better than the translation because it is less draped in decency, Anglo-Saxon restraint, and repression, but both versions are still fresh and powerful enough to account for the fact that several generations have responded to its vision, as well as for the fact that so much of it has engraved itself verbatim permanently in the memory. Whether its aphorisms have the depth and wisdom I once attributed to them is open to question. But there is little to apologize for in the object of my literary infatuation. It is not whom or what one loves that is important, as Proust tells us, but the great fact of loving itself. If anyone thinks Céline a literary ugly duckling and is disappointed in my lack of refinement in choosing him, that does not change the fact that it was the enthusiasm aroused in me by Céline's work that was primarily responsible for my going to see him. Possibly, as Proust's witty apologia for subjectivism suggests ("Let us leave pretty women to men without imagination"), I may have been suffering from an excess of romanticism and from a variety of psychic ills stemming from my Jewish identity, which, at the time, if permitted to survive at all, found itself particularly hard-pressed.

I was convinced that I had to do with a literary immortal, and it was for that reason above all that I went to see him. He caught some of the feeling surely from my letters to him. Struck by my attitude of literary reverence as we were talking one day in Denmark, Céline said to me with an inimitable trace of irony in his voice: "I belong to History!" To my mind, his claim to fame was much larger than this rather meager one. Everything that happens and especially what is recorded in the daily newspaper may be said to belong to history. Céline surely did that, but he also belonged to what was new and fresh and alive and indelible in literature. So I felt, at any rate, and feeling this way about him, I could hardly be dissuaded from taking up his urgent and repeated invitations to visit him.

For a long time I was minded to give Céline the benefit of every doubt, possible and impossible. Gide's hypothesis of a joking Céline, pressing Nazi ideas to such extremes that they would be laughed at, appealed to me. It enabled me to explore bookish analogies that might serve to exculpate him. The most ingenious perhaps was the one between *Bagatelles pour un massacre* and Defoe's *Shortest Way with the Dissenters*. Defoe was always one of Céline's favorite writers. When he learned, during my visit to him in Denmark, that one of the books I had brought to Europe with me to study in preparation for the fall semester was Defoe's *Memoirs of a Cavalier,* he indicated that he had read it and liked it. He had obviously read widely in Defoe. But had he read the pamphlet *The Shortest Way with the Dissenters*? I never asked him, and I'm sorry now that I didn't. It is only one of the questions I wish I had asked him. But precisely what is the relevance of that famous polemical tract by Defoe?

Defoe, a Dissenter himself, wrote a polemic aimed at Dissenters so violent that it was calculated to bring a reaction against its own extremism. The initial impulse of a number of High Churchmen (unfortunately for them preserved in print) had been to sympathize with the anonymous simplistic pamphleteer who proposed to cut the Gordian knot and deal with the problem of the Dissenters with direct murderous force. But soon some of the brighter adherents of the Establishment suspected that they might have fallen into a trap. Inquiry into the identity of the author of the offensive pamphlet revealed him to be a Dissenter himself who had, in his own words, assumed his fearsome merciless guise in order "to cut the throat" of the Anglicans. Defoe was sentenced to the pillory and very nearly had his ears cropped. This punishment did not keep him from celebrating the success of his ruse with a triumphant *Hymn to the Pillory*. It should be noted, however, that the incident, far from making him a hero or martyr in the eyes of his fellow Dissenters, whose cause he had found a way of serving with such imaginative ingenuity, only resulted in making Defoe suspect in the eyes of many of them ever afterward. They were not inclined to trust him much from that time on. By mimicking so successfully the secret murderous thoughts in the hearts of their enemies, he apparently had convinced many Dissenters that in his own heart of hearts he shared their malevolence. The life of the literary genius has never been an easy one. There is a deep, primitive, ineradicable instinct to trust the mask more than the face, and when one dons a frightening mask for any reason, one takes the risk of being torn apart by one's friends even if something tells them that the face behind the mask may be benign.

Defoe was apparently judged to be "too clever by half" by his fellow Dissenters, who cheered him in the Pillory but hesitated to trust a man capable of arguing the case against them so persuasively as to impose upon their opponents, who were not stupid, though they were a little slower than Defoe. But if this was what happened to Defoe, whose intentions were clear and who wrote in a long-recognized tradition of satire in a neo-classic age, what could Céline himself have expected, even if his satiric intention is granted, writing as he did in a declining romantic age and in a vein that he himself described as *delirium*? Some parallels between Defoe and Céline suggest themselves, of course. Thus, the enthusiastic reaction of fascist fellow travelers like Léon Daudet and Robert Brassilach to the extreme violence of the tone of *Bagatelles pour un massacre* may be analogous to the initial favorable reaction of the High Churchmen to the deadly proposals of *The Shortest Way with the Dissenters*. But the analogy soon peters out. Was Céline himself a Jew, as Defoe was a Dissenter? Not being a Jew and having flirted with anti-Semitism in earlier works like *L'Eglise* and *Mea Culpa,* could he have expected to be taken, at that moment in history, at other than face value? Besides, when Defoe's pamphlet had done its work of bringing disrepute on the Anglican establishment, the writer did not repeat himself but went on to something new. Not so Céline, whose *L'Ecole des cadavres* is an even more violent diatribe than *Bagatelles pour un massacre*. If he was being so subtle that he succeeded only in puzzling as gifted a reader as Gide, surely he had overreached himself far beyond what Defoe did. As Paul Valéry has noted, the iron law of literature is that what is valid for one alone is not really valid. If Céline had a secret intention recognized by no one but himself, then it must be said that he failed in his intention. If there had been anything in Gide's tentative hypothesis that the motive of *Bagatelles* was to caricature real racism (a guess to which I had taken an agnostic attitude in my introduction to *Death on the Installment Plan*), there was ample opportunity for Céline, in his letters to me between 1947 and 1949 and in his talks with me in the summer of 1948, to confirm the hypothesis. But he did not choose to do so. He may have come close to doing so in an early letter to me on 16 April 1947, in which he had written: "To reproduce the effect of spontaneous spoken life on the page, you have to bend language in every way—in its rhythm and cadence, in its words. A kind of poetry weaves the best spell: the impression, the fascination, the dynamism. *Then, too, you must choose your subject—not everything can be transposed. You have to lay back the flesh of your subjects—and this means terrible risks. But now you have all my secrets.*"

It is hard to say exactly what these enigmatic words mean. Yet when I went to talk to him face-to-face, it was perhaps as much as anything in the hope that he might be encouraged to elaborate and clarify such thoughts as seem to be half-concealed here: that writing had become little more than an aesthetic exercise in which words were used as materials but were not meant to be taken seriously. They were merely a means with which "to get a rise" out of the reader, in other words to gratify or provoke him. But instead of developing tantalizing suggestions such as this, he chose (like the young Ferdinand in *Death on the Installment Plan*) to "clam up" on subjects he must have known were of the utmost interest to a young Jew.

I later learned that the Germans, during the Occupation of Paris, had also found him an uncomfortable bedfellow. In an exhibit of French anti-Semitic writings organized by the Nazis in Paris in 1941, Céline's books were almost pointedly omitted, drawing a vehement protest from him. It may be argued that the indignation of this protest, too, could have been feigned for satirical reasons. But if Céline appeared even to the Nazis to be too disreputable and "loony" a fellow traveler to inspire much enthusiasm, there was no effort on their part to pillory him or to ostracize him. When the Germans were facing defeat in 1944 and were attempting to make provisions to protect those who were generally regarded as among their collaborators, they gave sanctuary to Céline in Sigmaringen along with Pétain, Laval, and many collaborators and officials of the Occupation. Had Céline chosen to remain in Paris through 1944, it is quite possible that in the heat of the moment he may have been executed or assassinated on the streets (as happened to his publisher Denoel), but if he had not been, if he had been imprisoned and tried instead, a way might have been found, as it was with Hamsun in Norway and Pound in the United States, to spare him. By choosing instead to act like one of the picaresque poltroons in *Journey to the End of the Night,* fleeing from the field of battle, he made it inevitable that he would be stigmatized by his countrymen for the rest of his life, as actually happened when his one-year prison sentence was suspended in 1951 and he was permitted to return to France.

Now, it is foreigners mainly who are striving to secure his literary reputation, which he has never wholly lost, just as once, a generation ago, it was an American and Jew like myself, who came forward to offer help, which he originally welcomed but eventually treated with suspicion and resentment. Céline, in the nature of the case, could hardly have repeated Defoe's feat in *The Shortest Way with the Dissenters,* even if he had intended to do so. The eighteenth century in England was not yet lost to a sense of shame when it felt that it had overshot the human mark. In that respect, it was quite unlike our own time, in which all concepts of decency, measure, restraint, "the inner check," have been so degraded that no suggestion can be regarded as completely beyond the pale or through its extremism capable of making anyone taking it seriously blush. As an example, Céline in *L'Ecole des cadavres* had hardly gotten through comparing the Jews to pestilential germs and suggesting that the proper way to treat them was to apply the same principles of antisepsis as were found useful in preparing surgical instruments for an operation—sterilize them by boiling not just for a few minutes, which are enough to get rid of most of the germs but not all of them, but for a full twenty minutes—when there appeared on Europe's scene human candidates prepared to carry out the experiment literally. Little wonder that Céline had noted in his speech on Zola in 1933 that literature had never been easier to write or harder to tolerate than in his time. The world of the twentieth century had "blown its top" so far as the most elementary humanity and conscience were concerned. It is said that at Céline's trial in absentia in Paris in 1951, when some of his more bizarre proposals were read aloud in the courtroom, they provoked laughter. But they were no laughing matter in 1938 or in 1943. For that matter, they can be a laughing matter at any time only for those who find that a bar against inciting murder of fellow human beings is the only intolerable inhibition left to explode, now that so many sexual taboos have been blown up. Pornography and anti-Semitism have for a long time shown strong affinities for each other, and they have sometimes been purveyed by the same persons. Now that pornography, through the new licentiousness without limits, has largely lost its "punch," anti-Semitism may be the only way left for getting kicks for those who cannot be happy unless they are ostentatiously throwing off the yoke of the moral law.

I always regarded my differences of opinion with Céline as honest ones (granting even, when pressed, that they were based on no absolute criterion but might stem from our different prejudices), and I proposed, when inquiry was made of me and in *The Crippled Giant* itself, to leave his punishment to his own conscience rather than to the law-courts. I regarded his postwar defense of his own conduct before and during the war as disingenuous at best. The actual harm that such polemical writings as his could do is debatable, but I would not advocate censorship of his opinions even if they did prove harmful. Unfortunately, Céline did not choose to return the compliment so far as recognition of my own right to freedom of opinion was concerned. He labored diligently though in vain to silence me after having invited me to write a book about him. It has been said that "toleration requires a sense of humor and an ability to mistrust oneself." For a time, it appeared to me that Céline and I possessed both of these qualities and that our relationship, despite everything, might prosper because of them. Certainly, Céline's humor (call it "black" or whatever) is one of the first characteristics I deeply appreciated in him (as my introduction to the 1947 New Directions edition of *Death on the Installment Plan* shows), and I thought I had also detected in him, during our correspondence, an ability to distrust himself. But there were evidently strict limits to his sense of humor when he felt himself threatened, and the prejudices to which he gave free rein in his "pamphlets" might have alerted me to the fact that he did not mistrust himself even a fraction as much as he mistrusted others (his epigraph for his *Homage to Zola* is "Men are mystics of death whom it is necessary to mistrust!"). This was especially true perhaps in relation to someone like myself whose clear image he was completely unable to grasp or to separate from the caricatures and stereotypes supplied to him by his melodramatic satirical imagination (Jew-Judas, American secret agent, suspect journalist and intellectual), with all of which he burdens the splintered personality whom he depicts in his *Entretiens avec le professeur Y.*

What he now seems to me to have been lacking more than anything else is what Whitman describes as "the antiseptic of the soul," namely faith in his fellow human beings. He once wrote me that in Europe the very stones seemed to drip venom. He himself was evidently early poisoned by doubt. He could not believe that, in writing of him as I did in my book, I meant him no harm, though I meant his ideas — whatever they were — no good. He obviously did not think that my plea that he be left to his own devices and his own conscience rather than suffer public punishment was sincere. And he could hardly credit the possibility that my account of him, far from arousing impulses to vengeance against him, might actually help to create some measure of understanding and compassion for him. He would never have admitted it, but the actual outcome of the publication of my book which he so much feared, far from wreaking the harm he anticipated and hysterically tried to prevent, may have helped to some degree in producing the favorable outcome of his trial, which permitted him to return to France and to produce, during the last ten years of his life, the trilogy dealing with World War II, which some critics at least (though I am not among them) regard as some of his best writing. He lived those last years of his life in peace, visited by occasional pilgrims and curiosity seekers, academicians and journalists. And that is an outcome which, if presented with a choice, I would have wished for him. I had no interest at any time in adding him to the world's much too long list of literary martyrs. If only for his *Journey to the End of the Night, Death on the Installment Plan,* and *The Life and Work of Semmelweis,* he had put me and all his readers deeply in his debt, and it was not my intention to return evil for all the good he had done me. And even his creative works of the second rank (*Guignols Band, Le Pont de Londres, Féerie pour une autre fois,* and so on) and his most outrageous polemics (*Bagatelles pour un massacre, L'Ecole des cadavres,* and *Les Beaux Draps*) are all worth reading. Even in his most benighted and delirious ravings there are redeeming flashes of wit and insight.

The world passes its judgment on men and books dispassionately, as the Latin has it, but it is in no hurry to do so, and it sometimes seems to speak (as the Indians used to say of the white man) with forked tongue. It is not easy to keep up with all that has been and is being said about Céline, not only in French but in many other languages, since he died almost a generation ago. Writers on Céline generally regard *The Crippled Giant* as a significant tribute to him and to his representative quality in the literature of the Western world in the twentieth century. Judging from the number of citations of passages from his letters to me, these seem to be regarded as the most revealing things he wrote about his literary aims to anyone.

The true complexity of my feelings, motives, and conclusions seems to grow plainer as the literature on Céline multiplies around the world. Because of my tortured and strenuous striving after fair-mindedness, detachment, and balance of judgment, my book has often been singled out for special attention. I would not be a writer if I were always completely satisfied with what my readers have found or not found in my book. But when I think I have some complaint to make, I try to recollect an interesting comment I have come across in a letter of Franz Rosenzweig to Stefan Zweig in 1928: "I have always suspected that our common writers' vice of never being satisfied with our readers — instead of marveling anew each time at the miracle that a complete stranger, completely unconcerned with us, should even bother to read what we have written — has its solid foundation in the gross discrepancy between the amount of time the writer spends in writing and the reader in reading. When I once complained of this to Buber he cited, to comfort me, the lasting influence we exert on our readers. This is true enough, but like all drafts on the future, it is only a solace, not a remedy for the present illness."

Having fortunately been spared long enough to see some of the future of *The Crippled Giant,* first published more than thirty years ago, I have found enough solace to satisfy me that whatever the verdict is, brought in by a remoter future, it can only be a just one.

Thirty-five years ago, in a state of confusion as to the meaning of my experience with Céline, I gave my essay on him a title designed to point to a mythic parallel between my adventure and that of Odysseus with the one-eyed giant Polyphemus. Now that I am approaching three-score years and ten (and do not feel quite out of the woods yet), I see it rather in the light of a quixotic quest undertaken in search of a quixotic author who himself has depicted a quixotic character (Courtial des Pereires) and who should have been greatly flattered to be compared as a creator to Cervantes or to his brain-child, Don Quixote. Neither the Homeric analogy nor the more modern one is precise, but both attest to the inevitability with which an extremely intense experience of reality is doomed to be assimilated by an individual to his knowledge of the greatest of literary classics. The literature we profess is neither pastime nor puzzle nor self-indulgent pleasure nor opportunity for intellectual display, though it is often treated as if it were simply one or another or a combination of these. It is probably nothing less than the world's most dangerous game. There may be only one thing more risky, and that is existence itself (from which we initially seek refuge in it). Like others before me, I may not have realized just what I was up to when I first undertook to leave a written trace upon the world, but since then, there has been nothing to do except live with the consequences, which more and more seem endless . . .

— 1983

Reminiscences of Robert Frost

FROST IS DEAD, has been for over fourteen years now, and swarms of poetasters, criticules, and pedants have been dancing delightedly on his grave. There have been veritable orgies of the most shameless character-assassination. The initial hierophant of these proceedings was the late Professor Lawrance Thompson, Frost's "official" biographer, but since he has departed his good work of decomposing a legend has been continued by others, and it is the indecent extremes to which some of these have gone in public places that have provoked me into setting down this record of my own all too few face-to-face meetings and talks with Frost. Perhaps it may help restore some balance to the picture and remind us that we have to deal with a man, not a monster. Professor Thompson was apparently hell-bent on entering literary annals in competition with Rufus Griswold, the chosen executor of Poe who became the executioner of his personal reputation and has reaped the contemptuous obloquy of Poe scholars for his pains ever since. Thompson's fulsome multi-volume catalogue of Frost's mortal and venial sins has encouraged others to vent their malice, entirely unmindful not merely of the well-known injunction against judgment in the Sermon on the Mount but of the saying of Rabbi Hillel (*Pirke Aboth*, II, 5) which preceded and perhaps inspired it: "Judge not thy fellowman until thou art come into his place!" Samuel Johnson said that in the last analysis no man is written up or down except by himself, and the traducers may eventually find that they have spat against the wind with the usual results.

Thompson's opus is part of a popular modern genre, the overstuffed, obese, voyeuristic biographical treatment to which Henry James, Marcel Proust, James Joyce, John Keats, and Emily Dickinson, among others, have been subjected. In a scientific age this has become a substitute for the novel and romance, which are in decline. It is inseparable from the inflation or deflation of the importance of its subject matter, and, far from being ancillary to aesthetic appreciation, is probably at odds with it. That is why many of those sensitive to literature have little interest in it and are, in fact, almost uniformly hostile to it. The late Philip Rahv, who had been prominent in the revival of interest in Henry James in the 1940s, was moved in the early 1970s to utter a protest against what had happened to James in Leon Edel's *five* volumes. On the publication of the fifth volume, *Henry James: The Master, 1901–1916,* Rahv wrote:

> That Edel makes too much of James, that he overestimates his im-
> portance in the most extravagant manner possible, that he is much
> too expansive, even rapturous, about him has been evident all along.
> . . . The excessive length of this biography is explained by its glut
> of detail of which much is only of minor interest. No wonder that
> the effect of far too many pages is that of supersaturation . . . After
> all, we are interested not in every casual person who came (James's)
> way, but only in his principal literary and social relationships.
> Moreover, the few happenings that might be regarded as "events"
> in his life are treated at inordinate length. . . .

Italo Svevo is a lucky writer in that his fine biographer, Furbank, has limited himself to less than 300 pages in treating, as his subtitle tells us, both "the man and the writer." After all, 300 pages were not too few to devote to the philosopher Schopenhauer. Why should any writer need more, unless the biographer is striving not to serve the interested reader who needs no persuasion about the importance of his subject but to put the subject in his place and to compete with him in imaginative appeal? It is not surprising to hear of some am-bitious, overreaching, competitive biographers who, in private, have expressed contempt for the subjects they professed to admire in public.

Boswell, it is true, produced a voluminous masterpiece, which has served gossip-mongers as a model, unfortunately, and Eckermann and Horace Traubel have produced hagiographies (with poets tak-ing the place of saints), but such whole-hearted enthusiasts are few, and they must not be sought among those whose enthusiasms are in-spired by their own opportunities and whose productions are of more interest to the bookseller than they are to literature. About the literary creators, anecdotal history may be the best, the kind that Diogenes Laertius wrote about the ancient philosophers and Vasari about the painters of the Renaissance.

The first time I heard Frost was in the Auditorium of the New School for Social Research in New York, where I was teaching a course in poetry. It was, as I recall, at the end of World War II. Of that occasion I remember an anecdote he told and an exchange after the lecture. The anecdote was about the time in the 1920s when psychologists divided all people into two types: extroverts and introverts, and then gave various signs by which people might judge as to which type they belonged. As Frost told the story, he had much trouble deciding which type he belonged to and vacillated between classifications until the real answer to the riddle suddenly came to him: "I'm neither an extrovert nor an introvert, just a plain vert from Vermont!"

I liked the clever turn of that story, its unassuming self-deprecation and playfulness, the very qualities of his poems which gave me pleasure and helped me to commit large numbers of them to memory. Later reflection made me see an additional characteristic quality in the story; that is what I should call its typically American "both-and" quality, which is also present in many of his poems which must be understood to say that the whole truth seems to be made up of seemingly contradictory halves and that to get it we must somehow manage to yoke these halves together instead of choosing between them, as a more logical "'either-or" philosophy might suggest. Try this idea out, for example, on "Mending Wall" in which a measure of truth inheres both in the liberal integrationist point of view: "Something there is that doesn't love a wall / That wants it down. . . ." and the old stubborn farmer's reiterated traditionalist saw: "Good fences make good neighbors," with its implication of inevitable separatism (cf. Kipling's "East is East, and West is West. . . ."). Try it out on "The Death of the Hired Man," where Mary's feminine sentiment and Warren's masculine hardness are incomplete without each other; both are true in a way, but neither is quite true, by itself. Try it even on a poem that puzzles many readers, "Provide, Provide." It's puzzling because only the cynical side of the argument is stated; the less cynical one is left to the reader's imagination. Even those alert to irony ("the Holy Ghost of this latter day," as Fitzgerald called it) are not prepared for such an extreme of irony, irony with a vengeance it may be called. I call the quality ("both-and") typically American, because we are particularly uncomfortable when called upon to make hard choices and think we may somehow escape them by combining together the incompatible and perhaps mutually exclusive.

In the conversation I had with Frost after his talk that evening, I was impressed with the directness, ease, and unpretentious approachability of his social manner. It was a continuation of the attitude on stage that won the audience over immediately. It could originate only in an integrity and unshakable self-confidence that had no need for masks or pretenses. Learning that I was a teacher myself, he asked me immediately if I did not think that making students memorize poems was still the most effective way of getting them to understand and appreciate poetry. At any rate, he had found that it was on the basis of his own experience in teaching, though we both knew in what low regard such "rote-memorization" was held in the pedagogy fashionable nowadays. But what did that matter, if it was really so. Hold on to the truth as you see it long enough, as he says in a poem somewhere, and the world is sure to come back to it in time.

I remembered that advice when I went to teach at the University of Chicago later in the 1940s and found that T. S. Eliot was very much "in," and Frost, while not quite "out," very much left alone with the implication that he was much too simple to be bothered with and could safely be left to adolescents, nativists, lazy readers, and even the Philistines who hated all other poetry. That got my back up, and I announced a lecture in the Harriet Monroe Poetry Room of the Library, the very citadel of modernity, entitled "One Reader's Reevaluation of Eliot and Frost." The point, I suppose, was that to love Eliot more it was not necessary to love Frost less, and it caused somewhat of an impression and even a stir, judging by the hostile reaction of some of my colleagues. I guess I was trying to apply Frost's own "both-and" approach, and I stepped on a lot of toes. Some of these belonged to snobs and some to logicians. Whitman had noted that people were "proud to get at the meaning of poems." Without meaning to, I offended pride and seemed to be threatening some substantial intellectual investments.

Some graduate students were more favorably impressed than my colleagues with my paradoxical thesis that Eliot's poetry was really easier that it seemed and Frost's more difficult. I remember a lecture in which I discovered some unexpected comparisons between such an "elementary" popular poem as "Stopping by Woods on a Snowy Evening" and *The Castle*, by Franz Kafka! I sent the notes of this talk to Frost but received no acknowledgment from him. Perhaps he found the indirection of my intellectual method suspect.

I did not see Frost again until I went to Brandeis University in 1948, where I headed for a time the Adult Education Program, of which a series of poetry readings was a feature. Our visitors included W. H. Auden, E. E. Cummings, Dylan Thomas, William Carlos Williams, Robert Lowell, Delmore Schwartz, and Karl Shapiro. But no one was better disposed to our young school or returned more often to read or speak to us than Frost. It was an important contribution to our morale, and our students and older "constituents" reciprocated the cordiality of his attention. He was the only poet aside from E. E. Cummings who was capable of filling the largest hall we could provide. William Carlos Williams, Auden, Dylan Thomas and the others all had their followings but did not compare in this respect with Frost and Cummings.

It was in connection with these visits that I saw Frost on the Brandeis campus, spoke to him on the phone (on one occasion he talked to me for half an hour about *The Book of Job,* which he told me he was rereading when I mentioned the fact that I was studying *A Masque of Reason* with a class), and visited him in his home on Brewster Street in Cambridge. It is a lasting regret that I did not take up his cordial invitation to my wife and me to visit him at his summer home in Ripton, Vermont. We had spent a very good evening after which he wrote in my copy of his *Collected Poems*: "To Milton Hindus, thanks for the evening I had with him on and off the stage at Brandeis, April 23, 1958 . . . Robert Frost." I am not sure now why I did not take up his invitation, since I found all my contacts with him pleasing and memorable, and I should certainly have increased my store of personal knowledge of him. In part, it was due to my lack of enterprise in traveling, and at that time a trip to Vermont seemed to me longer than it does now. In part, too, it was no doubt a result of the disillusion I had experienced in my unforgettable trip to Denmark in 1948 to spend a month talking to Louis Ferdinand Céline. The experience had resulted in my book *The Crippled Giant,* but it had taken a great deal out of me emotionally, and I was in no mood to come close again to "a great writer," even if I recognized that there was a world of difference between Frost and Céline and that the earlier experience was not likely to be repeated. Whatever the reason, I did not see Frost in his preferred surroundings and must content myself with memories of the times and places I did see him in.

The Brandeis campus is beautiful; in the early days when we had just taken it over from Middlesex and had not yet launched the extensive building program that has given us over eighty structures, it was more beautiful still. There were orchards and gardens, arbors, a wishing well, pleasant walks and prospects. Some of these have survived our "progress," some not. Frost and I were walking around the campus in one of the early years after 1948, and we came to a hill near the castle we had inherited from Middlesex, from which a broad wooded prospect stretched away. Frost stood looking at a grove of silver-barked trees and said, with no trace of vanity, I thought, but matter-of-factly, "There are some of my birches." And it was true. From a human point of view he had appropriated this part of nature.

In our eyes, birches would never be the same again as they were before he wrote the poem familiar to generations of schoolchildren. On that day, too, he surprised me when we were talking about Brandeis and especially about our faculty (which included from the beginning some well-known, even famous men) by taking no interest in anyone except Benny Friedman, our football coach, an all-American player in his student-days at the University of Michigan where he had been on the team that played against Red Grange's. Frost remembered listening to the radio broadcasts of some of the games in which Friedman had starred and the skill and braininess of his play (he is credited in histories of football with first developing the offensive power of the forward-pass) had made an unforgettable impression on Frost, who was evidently not a one-sided intellectual with a contempt for popular sports.

On a later occasion, I remember Frost "saying" his poem "Stopping by Woods" to a small group of us and indicating that he was willing to hear any questions or comments we cared to make about it. Whereupon one of my colleagues, a French poet, launched into a complex and elaborate explanation of why he thought Frost had closed the final (fourth) stanza of the poem with the repetition:

> And miles to go before I sleep,
> And miles to go before I sleep.

The poet spoke excellent English but with a heavy French accent. Frost heard him out patiently, then said: "But you don't understand. In English, we have an expression miles and miles. It's *that* I was thinking of when I repeated those lines." It sounds rude as I tell it now (and if Thompson or some of his reviewers had heard about it, they would no doubt find in it a confirmation of Frost's heartlessness and cruelty), but it was not in the least rude or heartless or cruel as I heard it. It was instructive.

Frost thought that poetry is what disappears in translation. That may not be wholly true, but it will do for a start, and it is corrective of the commonplace notion that ignores the power of language and settles upon more abstract and cloudy sentiment or sublimity of thought as an explanation. Hearing the poet's accent more than the line of his argument, Frost reminded him and us all that one of the deepest roots of a poem must be sought in the idiom peculiar to a language. Frost's comment may strike us at first as a simple joke, but the more we think about it the more serious and less simple-minded it seems. If my colleague's feelings were hurt by the abruptness of the reply (I don't know that they were), it would not have been because Frost was cruel but because my colleague was more subjective in his approach to the "game" of writing poetry as well as we can with the language we have at our disposal.

What being a poet in a country like America meant was conveyed in an anecdote I heard him tell once. He was going to Washington in the old days on a Pullman sleeper, and being unable to sleep on a moving train he found himself sitting in a parlor-car beside a man who kept talking through the night. It became clear that he was one of the more important businessmen of the country and that he was going to Washington to testify before a Congressional committee as an expert witness. He kept talking, and Frost listened until morning came; at the last moment the businessman showed a flicker of interest in who his patient companion might be and asked jovially, "What's your racket?" And Frost answered, "I write poems," whereupon the man's face fell in obvious disappointment and he said, "Hell, my wife does that!"

Frost told it as a funny story, and there was something funny about it, but I thought I understood something more than I had before about the two roads he had spoken of in his famous poem, the "well-travelled" one which was "the road not taken" and the "less-travelled" one, the choice of which had made "all the difference."

That the businessman felt that way about poetry was to be expected. More hurtful was the competitiveness, and envy which Frost encountered among his own kind. I heard from friends in Cambridge that Frost once walked into a party of poets and their friends and found himself with no one to talk to. After a while he left, being heard to say as he was leaving (or maybe being *said* to say): "The bastards!" For I have no doubt that the hostile attitudes to him and to everything he stood for and especially to his success, which have surfaced so frankly since his death and seized upon the Thompson biography as a rationalization, were becoming evident to him in his later years. One of the "young" has now delivered himself of the pronouncement that Frost was so bad a man that it must have taken a special tolerance to stand being in the same room with him. I can well believe that in certain rarefied coteries he was given "the silent treatment."

Everything is held against him nowadays, even his admitted good actions. Was he instrumental in freeing Ezra Pound from incarceration in St. Elizabeth's Hospital? Yes, but he spoiled it all supposedly by claiming too great credit for it. Well, I know that he told me about it, because I saw him soon after he came back from Washington where he saw Herbert Brownell, Eisenhower's Attorney General, about the matter, and I heard nothing from Frost that was boastful or that was not borne out by what I later learned from those most partisan to Pound, like Harry Meacham, who tells the sad story of Pound's St. Elizabeth's period in the fullest detail in *The Caged Panther*.

On one occasion in the early 1950s, I remember trying to draw him out on the subject of Whittaker Chambers, whose book *Witness* I had assigned to the students in one of my courses. Frost had read Chambers' book, but beyond indicating his agreement with me that the story of Chambers' family was as terrible as any in a Russian novel, he was noncommittal. Frost had once ironically inquired in his poem "New Hampshire": "How can we write the Russian novel in America so long as life goes on so unterribly?" Well, Chambers gave one answer to that rhetorical question. Frost did indicate that he was hoping to write a poem on the meaning of loyalty, which I took to be a reflection on the intelligence of those for whom it was only an empty word and not a reality. Whether he had ever been aware that Whittaker Chambers was a poet (included in Louis Zukofsky's Objectivist anthology of 1931), I don't know. Chambers mentions his own poetry briefly in telling how it was used to throw doubt upon his credibility and even sanity in the courtroom (a story of some cultural significance, comparable to Frost's anecdote about the businessman), but he makes very little of it.

On another occasion when I called for Frost at Brewster Street in Cambridge to take him to a reading at Brandeis where I was to introduce him, I found him suffering from a heavy cold, running a temperature of 102 degrees. His doctor had told him not to go out, and I was preparing in my mind the excuses I would make to the audience that was waiting for him. But he surprised me. He had not missed a lecture engagement in 40 years, he told me, and he would not begin with Brandeis. He came, warmed to his task as he went along and, instead of cutting the reading short, as I had prepared the audience to expect by telling them of his fever, he went on for about an hour and a half, doing "encore" after "encore" to please his hearers who asked for their favorite poems. At the end he seemed more vigorous than at the beginning. He was then in his middle 80s.

It was on that occasion that he told me of plans he had to fly to various sections of the country that wanted to hear him read his poetry. I had a momentary twinge of concern about the chances he was taking in relying so much on air travel (which was not quite as much taken for granted then as it is now), and when I hinted at my feelings his imagination was immediately touched as he could see himself going down in a plane crash: "That wouldn't be pretty, would it?" and he made a face about it. His face was expressive, but strong rather than sensitive. His large, weighty, impressive head in his later years was gray and somewhat close-cropped. In his early years, his hair had been long and romantic-looking; he had been very handsome. His appearance was unmistakably individual without being eccentric. His being a working farmer was no pose, though I heard him poke fun (at himself or his neighbors or both) by telling how strange it seemed to some of his more conventional townspeople to see him occasionally milking his cows at midnight. His neck was short, and markedly thick, as Schopenhauer says the necks of geniuses should be to keep a good blood supply flowing to their brains.

He was a great reader (or, as he put it, "sayer") of his own poetry, in this respect resembling both Eliot and Williams. He did not intone his verses as I heard Pound do. His style of reading, as of writing, was an indissoluble combination of the artful and the natural. It was American, and more specifically New England, speech that we heard, but it was *measured* speech in which no syllable or accent was slighted or deprived of its due. He neither understated nor exaggerated the feeling — the two ways in which readings may go wrong. He clearly showed how poetry was more than merely an art for the eye and brain; in its fullness, it appealed to the ear and heart as well. If its appeal was less than fourfold, it was to that extent incomplete. And the thing the poet wrote on was only incidentally paper; more deeply, it was the memory of his readers. It is not surprising that he should have emphasized the role of memory in testing the appreciation of poetry.

The worst substantive criticism of Frost was that made by his initial influential discoverer and impresario, Pound, who later said of his popular protégé: "he sank of his own weight." That was not really true, though one could see what Pound meant. Humor was not Frost's strong suit, any more than it was that of greater poets like Wordsworth and Milton. I remember his telling me once about a party he had attended at which Irwin Edman (who relaxed from teaching Plato at Columbia by writing verses for *The New Yorker*) had said pleasantly, "Good fences make good burglars!" Frost had turned the remark over and over in his mind without really understanding it; only when it was pointed out to him that the sophisticated city slicker had intended to pun on the word "fences" (meaning receivers of stolen goods) did he grasp the joke (not much of a joke, but still . . .) in an embarrassed way.

Yet he appreciated joking and often tried to make jokes himself, even if, (like Milton's) they were a little ponderous, as when he suggested to our students (he later incorporated the suggestion in a quatrain) that the atomic bomb might have some real use if it could blow Shakespeare out of the English language so poor "fellers" like himself might have a chance. It sounded subversive at first blush and was really a neatly turned compliment. Again, there is the little poem in which, reversing the prophet who envisioned swords being turned into ploughshares, he tells how in the field one day he inadvertently stepped on a hoe which promptly struck him "in the seat of the pants," thus suggesting that Isaiah may have been unduly optimistic. The concluding couplet is a Byronesque rhyme:

> The first tool I step on
> Turns into a weapon.

More successful examples of his humor are the genre sketches in which his sense of drollery penetrates all of the material and does not attempt to concentrate itself in one or two words. Good examples of this mode are "A Hundred Collars" from *North of Boston* and the later and more celebrated "Witch of Coös."

More characteristic perhaps is his tragic end-of-the-world vein in which the joke that is played is by nature at the expense of the hopes of man. It is illustrated by "Fire and Ice," "Once by the Pacific," "Desert Places," and "Acquainted with the Night." His tragi-comic tone finds perfect embodiment in the concluding couplet of "Once by the Pacific":

> There would be more than ocean water broken
> Before God's last "Put out the light!" was spoken.

The pessimism of this bleak vision makes him eminently a twentieth-century voice, a whole world away from the optimism of Longfellow's "Psalm of Life": "Tell me not in mournful numbers / Life is but an empty dream . . ." He is even far removed from Whitman's modified optimism, which may be summed up in the transcendental individualistic message that, paraphrasing Longfellow:

> I am real, I am earnest,
> And the grave is not *my* goal . . .

Yet, in another sense, he continues the work of his New England predecessors, especially Thoreau, and we do not wonder that he chose for the title of his first book (published not in America but in England) *A Boy's Will,* which comes from the refrain of Longfellow's poem *My Lost Youth.* It was this aspect of piety toward the provincial past which probably made rebels against Puritanism and the genteel tradition like H. L. Mencken regard him with suspicion as a potential spokesman for the booboisie. Mencken described him, in a phrase which mischievously sticks even now, as a "Whittier without the whiskers." He could probably envisage him eventually reading a poem at a presidential inauguration.

But Mencken's assessment was nevertheless mistaken. Frost was a patriot with a difference. His pessimism eventually enabled him to siphon off the soupçon of sentiment and sweetness that for some tastes had spoiled some of his early poems, e.g. "The Tuft of Flowers," which Pound didn't mention in his review of *A Boy's Will* and which predictably became immediately popular with the anthologists. It is the dryness, objectivity, depth, and resolute refusal of easy sentimentality which makes "The Gift Outright" (which Kennedy asked him to read at his inauguration) one of the very few tolerable patriotic poems ever written in America.

Frost was a strange combination. Rahv's well-known distinction between "paleface" and "redskin" writers in America is perfectly useless, applied to him. He was both, and he was neither. More applicable perhaps is a subtle passage in Rahv in which he tells us that "a close observer of the creative process once finely remarked that the honor of a literature lies in its capacity to develop 'a great quarrel in the national consciousness.' " This formulation, though he didn't intend it, can hardly help but remind us of Frost's "lover's quarrel with the world." (Yvor Winters, in his wrongheaded essay on Frost, seems to me to have completely misapprehended the meaning of this self-description, as he misapprehended much else in Frost.)

Frost's current detractors make much of his supposed "campaign" to get the Nobel Prize. I never heard him say a word about it myself, though journalists were discussing it in the press, and I remember my own feeling that it would distinctly raise the level of esteem in which the literary prize was held (before he died it had gone to Steinbeck, Pearl Buck, and Sinclair Lewis), if it had been awarded to Frost (or, for that matter, Dreiser, Fitzgerald, or Pound). No prize could have possibly added luster to Frost's fame. He had long ago passed the most stringent test of a poet proposed by Whitman: his country "had absorb'd him as affectionately as he absorb'd it." The failure of a foreign academy to elect him was its own failure, nothing more. It reminds me of the inscription on the bust of Molière which greets the visitor to the building in Paris which houses the Académie Française: "We are not lacking from his glory, but he is missing from ours." A graceful way for the forty "Immortals" to acknowledge their own fallibility and lack of discernment. It is not in the power of any intellectual or academic élite to bestow immortality; they can only recognize it where it exists, and they often don't do even that. Many of them didn't in the case of Frost; some still don't.

The failure of foreigners to appreciate fully the distinction of Frost may only be a confirmation of his own observation that poetry is what vanishes in translation. In any case, the appreciation of foreign writers is often little more than an echoing of hearsay or an expression of snobbery. This may be true even in the case of those as manifestly great as Keats, Goethe, or Pushkin. Worse still, it may be a response to an easily discerned trick of style or the expression of a mood which mirrors that of the writer's immediate contemporaries. This might go a long way toward explaining the international vogue which was once Byron's and is still Hemingway's among ourselves.

Frost's "letter to the world" is now committed to hands he cannot see, our hands. It devolves upon those of us who value the English language and American speech and wit to see that the letter does not miscarry in our generation because of those who would cast aspersions on his achievement by impugning the character of the man who produced it (for it is inconceivable to me how that achievement could be linked to the scarecrow they seek to summon up in our imagination).

As for the homely simplicity that seems to disturb some deep readers today (rumor had it that it disturbed members of the Swedish Academy who thought that they recognized in him the kind of unexceptionable but modest peasant poet not at all unusual in literatures with which they were familiar), it reminds me that Franz Schubert had to wait for a very long time to find his proper place in the classical canon, because to superficial "quick deciders" (the expression is Scott Fitzgerald's), his music sounded no different from that of hundreds of other moderately talented Viennese composers. Time may catch up with such laggards eventually and make them take thought about what they have missed. But those lucky enough to be smitten with beauty or wisdom need not wait so long. They realize at once when they have encountered sounds or thoughts which stir them so deeply they think they can never forget them as long as they live. And it is a comfort when this intimation proves to be true. They don't forget.

He was my own idea of the ideal teacher, one who spoke with authority because his own work lent weight to his words. An exceptional amount of what I heard from him has stayed with me. But I realized that he did not meet everyone's expectations of what a teacher ought to do. I heard some criticism of him, which I found it difficult to understand or sympathize with. There was no doubt that his own work came before anything else, and therefore those who expected him to do it for them or for some of his wisdom to rub off on them by contagion might have been disappointed. He warned young teachers who, like himself, were productive, that teaching might become an excuse to neglect their own work. He would say cryptically: "Don't get stuck in the flypaper!" The best teaching was by example anyway. Describing his duties at a college in which he was in residence, he said that he was expected to be a "poetic radiator." He probably would have agreed with Kant that only properly prepared and intelligent students could be reached by a teacher. Kant used to say that the most brilliant ones would take care of themselves and that the dullards were beyond help; it was the middle group of eager and enthusiastic learners that he could help. It was the same group, I think, that Frost inspired as well. My own experience and memories suggest it.

In 1962, not long before his death, Frost wrote in anticipation of it a set of typical, playful verses entitled "Away." The last stanza goes as follows:

> And I may return
> If dissatisfied
> With what I learn
> From having died.

What some of us who admired him greatly have learned since his death from the posthumous assault on his person is to be more cynical about the world than he himself ever was. As for his detractors, it is not his ghost that they have to fear as much as it is his admirers. According to Auden, writing on the death of Yeats in 1939, a poet when he dies "becomes his admirers." That is, I suppose, a metaphor. But it is true that we who remain and feel that we have benefited from his existence and labors, and that his life, however long it was (almost 89 years), was not nearly long enough so far as we are concerned, may feel a responsibility of bearing witness on his behalf as both man and poet and being guardians of his well-earned renown.

—1979

Index

177

Printed December 1987 in Santa Barbara & Ann Arbor
for the Black Sparrow Press by Graham Mackintosh
& Edwards Brothers Inc. Design by Graham Mackintosh.
This edition is published in paper wrappers; there are
250 cloth trade copies; & 100 copies have been handbound
in boards & are numbered & signed by the author.

Photo by Joseph Attie

Essays: Personal and Impersonal is the fourteenth book by Milton Hindus. Among his others are a book of his own poems, two books on Walt Whitman, two books on Marcel Proust, two books on Charles Reznikoff, as well as books on F. Scott Fitzgerald, Maurice Samuel, the immigrant Jews of the Lower East Side of New York, and the Jews of eastern Europe in the 19th and early 20th centuries. His *Crippled Giant*, the first book on Céline in English, has been described by scholars as a classic and has been translated into French and Japanese. He has been awarded the Walt Whitman Prize by the Poetry Society of America. He taught for 33 years at Brandeis University and was Edytha Macy Gross Professor of Humanities at the time of his retirement. For briefer periods he has taught at the University of Chicago, UCLA, NYU, The New School for Social Research, and Hunter College. He has served as an Editor of *The Encyclopaedia Judaica* and has been a contributor to the German *Lexikon der Weltliteratur im 20 Jahrhundert* and the American *Dictionary of Literary Biography*. Articles and reviews by him have appeared in *The New York Times Book Review*, *The Atlantic Monthly*, *Le Monde* (Paris), *The Jerusalem Post*, and many other periodicals here and abroad.